Puffin Books

UNDER THE MOUNTAIN

When Theo and Rachel Matheson head for Auckland to
spend a fortnight with their uncle and aunt, they are
prepared for the usual entertainments that the city can
provide. But their relatives have curious neighbours who
seem to take an unnatural interest in the red-haired twins.
And once they meet the extraordinary Mr Jones, their
holiday begins to take a course of its own.

Beneath supposedly extinct volcanoes giant creatures
are waking from a spellbound sleep of several thousand
years. Their goal is the destruction of the world. Time
is running out. The Matheson twins, chosen to oppose the
monsters, know themselves to be as fallible as any other
eleven-year-olds . . .

This marvellously exciting fantasy novel, with its
enjoyable setting of present-day New Zealand, will be
specially appreciated by readers of ten and over.

Also in Puffins, *The Halfmen of O* and *The World Around
the Corner*.

MAURICE GEE

Puffin Books

Puffin Books, Penguin Books Ltd, Harmondsworth, Middlesex, England
Viking Penguin Inc, 40 West 23rd Street, New York, New York 10010, U.S.A.
Penguin Books Australia Ltd, Ringwood, Victoria, Australia
Penguin Books Canada Ltd, 2801 John Street, Markham, Ontario, Canada L3R 1B4
Penguin Books (N.Z.) Ltd, 182–190 Wairau Road, Auckland 10, New Zealand

First published in New Zealand by Oxford University Press 1979
Published in Puffin Books 1982
Reprinted 1982, 1983, 1985

Printed and bound in Great Britain by
Cox & Wyman Ltd, Reading
Filmset in Sabon by Rowland Phototypesetting Ltd,
Bury St Edmunds, Suffolk

CONTENTS

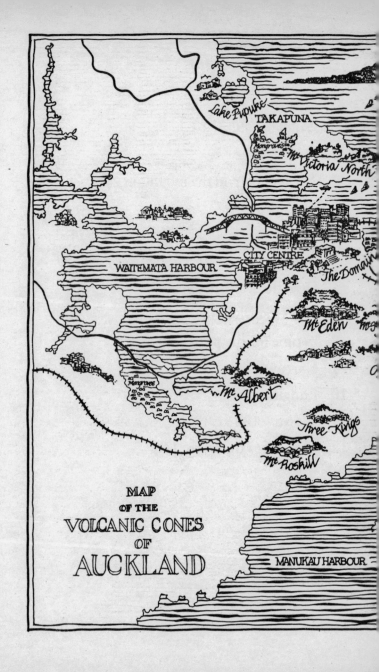

MAP
OF THE
VOLCANIC CONES
OF
AUCKLAND

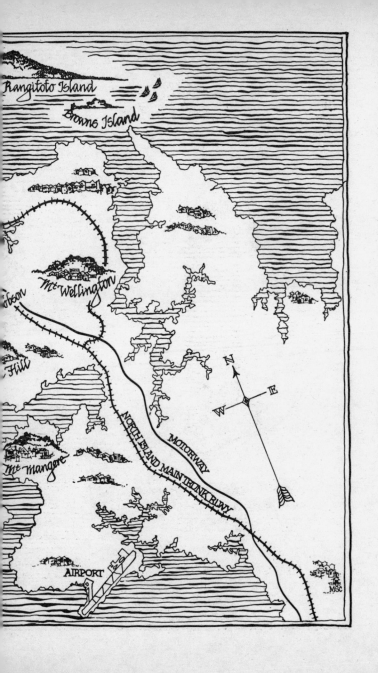

For Emily and Abigail

PROLOGUE

One afternoon on a farm outside a small town in the King Country two children wandered into the bush and were lost. They were twins, a brother and sister, three years old. Their father was mending fences. For more than half an hour he did not notice they were gone. When he looked up and saw the empty paddock, the bush, the brown cold river, he had the dreadful feeling that his children were lost forever.

He ran up the river bank, calling their names. He plunged into the bush. For an hour he searched, growing more frightened, more frenzied. Then he ran back to his truck and roared across the fields to his house. He shouted to his wife in the kitchen, rang the police, rang neighbours; and by late afternoon a hundred men and women, many with dogs, were searching the river banks and the bush by the farm. They found nothing. The sun went down behind the black hills west of the town. Darkness came. Winter is hard in this part of the North Island. The morning paddocks are white as though under snow. A frost of ten degrees was expected that night.

One man in the town had not heard of the search. He was just passing through. He was an old man and did not look as if he would have been much help anyway. The waitress at the hotel brought him his soup. She slopped it on the tablecloth and apologized. 'It's those poor little dears out in the bush,' she explained. 'I just can't keep my mind off them.'

'What little dears?' asked the man.

'The Matheson twins. You haven't heard? They wandered away from their father into the bush. Only three they are. Rachel and Theo Matheson. They'll freeze to death, the poor little lambs.'

'Is somebody searching?' The man put his spoon down. The quickness of his movement startled the waitress – and his face was suddenly younger than it had been.

'Oh yes,' she said. 'More than a hundred people. Police and forestry gangs. And dogs. They've even had a helicopter. But they can't do much in the dark. I've seen those children, here in town. Such bright wee things. Little redheads, they are.'

'Red-heads?' The man pushed his chair back. 'How do I get to the farm? Which way? No, never mind.' His face went pale, his eyes closed for a moment.

'Are you all right, sir?'

He said nothing, but in a moment stood up. 'Yes, I've got it. I can help.' He walked to the door.

'Sir,' the waitress cried, 'your soup, your dinner.' She ran after him to the foyer. But when she came into it he was not there. The glass doors were still and the stairs empty. She peered into the office, behind the sofa. Nothing. He had vanished. That was impossible. 'Oh dear,' she said, and sat down. She felt quite faint.

Out in the bush the Matheson twins were lying side by side on a bank of fern. They were too cold, too weak, to cry out, too weak even to whimper. They could not see each other in the dark, but they held hands tightly, and whispered from time to time for their parents to come. Theo first, then Rachel, they drifted to sleep. As they lay there, damp and still, the small amount of warmth left in their bodies drained away. A searching policeman crashed by, twenty metres down the bank. His torch lit the trunks of trees. Further on he stopped to call their names. Deep, deep in their sleep, they heard no sound.

The policeman went on, calling now and then to the searchers up and down the hill from him. A short while later they came together in a clearing by a stream.

'Nothing?'

'Nothing.'

'They'll never survive.'

'Look,' the policeman cried.

A light like a flame was moving in the trees, so bright it made them hide their eyes. It floated high above the ground, turning like a mist through the trunks.

'What is it?' They ran over the clearing, but as they ran it vanished, and they stood bewildered in the weak glow of their torches.

In that same instant, deep back in the bush, the light came down beside Rachel and Theo Matheson. It covered them like a blanket, flowed round and under them, soft and honey-coloured, drew down and dulled itself. Warmth flowed into the limbs of the sleeping children. They smiled and murmured. All night they slept as though in their beds at home. They dreamed happy dreams. The light lay still and warm over them, murmuring like a hive of bees.

Greyness came through the black night of the bush. Trucks and cars roared into the Matheson farm. Policemen, farmers, gathered for a second day of the search. Dogs barked. A helicopter chattered down the valley from the town.

In the bush the light in the fern patch stirred, concentrated itself. Suddenly it vanished. An old man stood beside the sleeping children. He knelt and touched their faces. 'Twins,' he murmured, 'twins.' He touched their red hair. 'Yes, yes, our colour.' He looked into their minds. 'And with the gift. They will be the ones.' He knelt for a long time, watching them. 'But will they be grown in time?'

The twins stretched, woke, sat up. They stared at him.

'You are safe, children,' he said. 'Someone will come for you soon and take you home.'

They stared.

'You will know who I am one day. Ten years. Maybe sooner. I will call you when you have to do your task.'

They did not understand. They smiled at him.

'I'm hungry,' Rachel said.

'Yes, yes, of course. I'll send someone. Now go to sleep. And remember me.'

Obediently, they lay back in the ferns and closed their eyes. They slept.

The man watched them for a moment longer. He touched them again on the brow. 'Poor things. Poor chosen ones. You must be brave.' He stood up, bowed his head; and vanished.

A moment later one of the farmers searching along a stream bed noticed his dog stop dead, as though it had walked into an invisible wall. It turned at right angles, quivered, gave an odd yelp. Then it dashed away up the hill. 'Come back,' the farmer yelled, 'I'll take your hide off.' He thought the dog must have scented a pig. He ploughed up the hill after it, falling behind. Then he heard excited barking. 'He's baled something up.' Two other men joined him. But it was not a pig. The dog had stopped beside a patch of fern. In that wet frozen bush it was oddly dry. They peered into it. And there, sleeping, warm and safe, their hands still clasped together, were the red-headed twins, Rachel and Theo Matheson.

The men lifted them up, wondering at the miracle, and carried them down through the bush to their parents' farm.

At the hotel the old man ate his breakfast. A phone rang and a moment later the waitress rushed in.

'They've found them,' she cried. 'They're safe.'

'Who?'

'The twins. The Matheson twins.'

'Oh, them,' the old man said. 'Will you bring my coffee?'

She thought him very hard-hearted. She did not notice how he smiled as he ate.

1. MAAR

The railcar clattered through the yards and rolled along at the side of a platform that Rachel and Theo thought would never end. They understood how much bigger a city was than their country town and they peered into the faces sliding by in the hope of seeing one that belonged to them.

'I wonder if they forgot.'

'There,' Rachel cried, 'it's Ricky.'

They were first out on the platform, lugging their heavy bags.

'Hi, kids,' Ricky yelled, coming at them and grabbing at their hair. 'Let me warm my hands.'

'Joke,' Rachel said. They had stopped being amused by remarks about their red hair. But they could not be offended by Ricky. He was too good-humoured.

'Where are your bags? Is that all you've got?' He lifted the suitcases as easily as if they had been filled with kapok. 'Come on. Wait till you see what I'm driving you home in.'

It was a beach buggy, with huge fat tyres, flaring mudguards, and red flames painted on the bonnet. 'I built it myself,' Ricky said. 'Took me more than two years. She'll do 130. Jump in.'

They climbed up and Ricky threw their bags in the back and leaped into the driver's seat. 'Course, I'm not allowed to do more than seventy with you kids on board.' They roared out into the traffic and ducked and dived through the streets of downtown Auckland. 'Good trip?' Ricky yelled.

'Rachel was homesick after five minutes.'

'I was not. I was looking at the scenery.'

'Some scenery. Cows and sheep. We can see those on the farm. This is better.' He waved at the wharves and tall buildings. The buggy chugged along the motorway and up on to the harbour bridge – and Rachel had to admit the view was exciting. The city came down to the sea, the wharves jutted out, ships lay in the harbour – and out beyond the North Shore, Rangitoto turned dark as the sun went down behind the western ranges. Rachel stared at the island.

'It's a volcano,' she said. 'Or was. I read about it. Rangitoto means bleeding skies.'

'Hey, no kidding,' Ricky said. 'I've been out there a dozen times but I never knew that.'

'I think it looks sinister.'

'There are lots of volcanoes round here. Extinct ones, I mean. Those little ones over there – that's North Head and Mount Victoria. And you can see Mount Eden if you take a look behind.'

They went through the toll gates on the North Shore side of the bridge and drove along the motorway past mangrove swamps into Takapuna. Ricky kept at seventy. 'I could have really wound her up along there,' he grumbled. They passed tree-lined streets leading to the sea and then turned away from it and drove down a right-of-way to a house standing on the edge of a small round lake.

'There you are,' Ricky said. 'You can fish from the bedroom windows.'

The house seemed made of glass with only ribs of concrete holding it together. Part of it jutted over the water. Curtains of different colours hid the interior. Rachel and Theo stared at it nervously. It was so different from their own old wooden house, so rich-looking. But they were excited too. It was something to have an uncle who owned a house like this, even if he did make plastic toys that broke as soon as you looked at them.

Ricky blew the horn and Aunt Noeline came running out. 'Twinnies,' she cried, throwing her arms round them. They had learned to put up with the name. She was very kind. After she had finished hugging them she took them inside. The house was split-level. They followed her up wide stairs to their bedrooms, feeling rather like goldfish in a bowl.

'I'll leave you to unpack,' Aunt Noeline said. 'Then we can have tea and a good old talk. Your Uncle Clarry will be home by then.' Ricky brought their bags up and put them in their rooms.

It took Rachel only a few minutes to get all her clothes into her drawers. She laid her brush and comb and toilet bag out on the dressing table. Then she pulled back the curtains over the end wall and found it was mostly glass. She was exactly above the place where the land met the water. Night was coming on quickly and lights were showing in the houses round the lake. Several small boats with coloured sails moved towards a landing place on the opposite shore. Seven or eight houses away, on a sloping lawn, under trees, two people were sitting on a bench facing the lake. They were hard to see because it was growing dark, and harder it seemed because they wore dark clothes. But it was a pleasant scene: two people – she strained her eyes – two old people, sitting close together as the last light of the day faded from the sky. She felt she could write a poem about it.

Ricky's voice rose from somewhere in the lower levels of the house. 'Hey Theo, come and see this.'

She heard her brother run down the stairs. A moment later a scraping sound came from below her and a splash of water. She peered down. Ricky and Theo were paddling a two-man canoe on to the lake. She opened part of the wall of glass.

'Hi,' she yelled, and Theo waved his paddle.

She was a little put out that Ricky had not called her. The canoe went straight out, then turned round to the left and vanished behind a curve in the shore. Rachel sighed. She would have loved to have been out there. The lake looked so still, so peaceful, with the last glow of sunset making pink reflections on its surface. But in a moment that was gone, the water suddenly looked very deep, very secret. Around its edge the houses seemed private, as though the people living in them had locked themselves away. Rachel shivered. She looked at the lawn where the old people had been sitting. But they were gone. Perhaps all the shouting had been too much for them. There were no lights in their house. It was cut off from the others round the lake by patches of waste-land covered with gorse and manuka.

The canoe came into sight, making along the shore towards home. Theo saw her standing in her window and saluted. She ignored him. She was, she admitted it now, a little bit homesick. At this time of day she was usually in the milking-shed hosing the yard for her father, or in the kitchen setting the table while her mother clattered around at the bench, and though neither was a job she enjoyed she found herself longing for them now – longing for her parents, the kitchen, the farm. Here she was, stuck in this spooky place with people she hardly knew. She felt like crying.

Then Aunt Noeline called her. She hurried down to the dining-room. Uncle Clarry had come home. He gave her a bear-hug. 'Well, how's the bush-fire blonde? My word, your brains must be sizzling in there.' Ricky and Theo came in and soon they were all sitting at the table eating a meal of chips and steak and lettuce salad and ice cream and peaches. Rachel decided that all that had been wrong with her was hunger.

'Ricky,' she said, 'next time you take me.'

'As long as you don't fall out,' he grinned.

'And don't yell so much either. You chased those people inside.'

'Which people?'

'In that funny old house along the lake. The one with the spiky roof. You were yelling so loud.'

'Huh,' Ricky said. 'Wilberforces. They're a pair of weirdos. You know, I've never seen the lights on in their house. I guess they just go to bed.'

'Don't you go bothering them,' Uncle Clarry said.

'Not me. I'll leave that to Old Jonesy.'

'Who's he?' Rachel asked.

'Jonesy? An old guy who lives round here – a couple of streets away. He hangs around the Wilberforces' place. Kind of spying on them.' He laughed. 'We've got our share of looneys in this town.'

'Don't you talk about Mr Jones like that,' Aunt Noeline said. 'He's a very nice old man. He brings me vegetables from his garden. He brought me some peas yesterday.'

'He's a bit nosey,' Uncle Clarry said, 'but he knows a thing or two, that old bloke.'

When dinner was finished Ricky showed them the garage. It took up most of the space under the house. There was room for Ricky's buggy and two other cars besides. On a lower level, close to the water, a boat sat on a trailer. It was a fibre-glass run-about, orange and white, with the name *Sea Lady* on its side in chrome-plated letters.

Ricky patted the motor. 'Pushes her along at forty knots. I'll take you for a spin one day. In the sea though. We don't take her on the lake.'

'Are there any fish in the lake?'

'Nothing worth eating. They tried to stock it with trout a while back but they didn't seem to take.'

'Maybe it's the smell,' Rachel said.

'Smell?'

'Well, you know, there's a funny . . .'

'I can't smell anything.' Ricky was offended. 'They used this for the water supply once for the whole North Shore. So it could hardly smell. I mean, it might be a bit polluted, everything is now. But there's no smell. I live here. I should know.'

'I'm sorry,' Rachel said. 'It was just when I opened the window of my room I thought I got a whiff of something.'

'Me too,' Theo said, 'when we were on the lake. It was very faint,' he said apologetically. 'A bit like . . . it's hard to say.'

'Rotten cabbages,' Rachel said.

'Hey, come off it,' Ricky cried.

'I'm sorry, Ricky. I can't smell it now.'

'Me neither,' Theo said. They avoided looking at each other.

'Well, you'd better not let Dad hear you talking about smells, that's all I say. He thinks this place is Buckingham Palace.'

'Ricky, can we take the canoe out now?' Rachel asked. 'You and Theo went out but I didn't have a turn.'

'Sure. Take it any time.'

The canoe was pulled up on the lawn below Rachel's window. They launched it and Theo held it steady while Rachel climbed in. Then he pushed off and jumped into his seat. They paddled until they were out of the light from the house.

'This is great.'

'Theo, there is a smell. I'm not imagining it.'

'I know. I can smell it now. It's stronger out here. Must be weed. Or dead fish.'

'It didn't look polluted. Why do you think Ricky can't smell it? Or Uncle?'

'Because they live here. They're used to it. Like Rotorua.'

'Well, I don't feel like touching the water.'

'Come on, Rachel, we don't have to swim in it. We swim in the sea. Let's go across to the other side.'

But they stopped in the middle of the lake and sat quietly in the canoe listening to the sounds of voices from the landing place where car lights showed some men fastening a yacht to the back of a jeep.

'What's that rumbling noise?'

'Cars up on the road.'

It was strange to be in so dark a place, so enclosed by darkness, yet ringed with lights and city noises. There was a fainter sound too, a rhythmical distant hiss that must come from the sea.

'We're in the darkest place,' Theo said. 'And higher than the sea. I wonder how this lake got here.'

Rachel looked at the lights. Off to the west was a long low building like a hospital, and northwards a tall block of flats. She made out tiny figures in the rooms. When she turned she saw Uncle Clarry too, talking into the phone. His house threw more light than any of the others. Where the curtains were closed it glowed in different colours. It looked, she thought, like a flying saucer ready to take off. Beside it the lawns had an artificial green.

She found the Wilberforces' house further along the shore. The glow from Takapuna outlined its roof. She made out spikes on the gable ends but the rest of it was hidden by trees.

'Why do you think they never have their lights on?'

'Who?'

'The Wilberforces.'

'Maybe they go to bed, like Ricky said. Or maybe they watch television in the dark.'

'Yes . . .' She was not convinced. 'It must be awful being old.'

'It's pretty awful being young when your sister keeps getting morbid.'

At that moment Aunt Noeline opened a window and yelled into the dark, 'You twins come back. It's getting late.'

'She wants the whole of Auckland to know.'

'Don't answer her.'

'Why not?'

'It's too quiet out here.'

They started to paddle back. Theo steered the canoe at the shore several hundred metres along from Uncle Clarry's house.

'Why are you going this way?'

'It's fun zipping through the reeds.'

She was going to protest – they would have to go past the wasteland by the Wilberforces' place. But Theo would be impatient so she kept quiet. She was very nervous. The dark, the stillness, were scary. She tried to concentrate on her paddling. Soon they were close to the shore and in the reeds. The canoe raced through them with a hiss.

'See?' Theo said.

They passed into the deep shade out from the wasteland. The trees on the low muddy bank at the foot of the Wilberforces' lawn approached and bent over them. Suddenly something tugged at Rachel's hair. She gave a small scream.

'What is it?' The canoe slowed down and rocked in the water.

'My hair caught on a branch. It's all right now.' She looked nervously at the house. The animal shapes of trees crouched on the lawn. Between two of them she saw the dull gleam of windows and a faint bluish light marking the shape of a doorway. In that rectangle of light something moved.

'Theo,' she hissed, 'look.'

'What?'

'The house. The door.' A huge black figure stood there.

22

'Who is it?'

'Him. Mr Wilberforce. It must be.'

They sat very still. And the shape in the door remained equally still. At last Theo whispered, 'He's big, isn't he? Must be more than two metres.'

'Is he watching us?'

'It's too dark.'

Quietly, quickly, they paddled away. Soon, behind them, they heard a door thud shut. They reached Uncle Clarry's house and pulled the canoe up on the lawn. Aunt Noeline called out of the window. 'Come on, you two, I want you to ring your mother. Then it's bed. You've had a big day.'

They went inside gratefully. On the phone to her mother Rachel was close to saying she wanted to come home. But Theo was bright and breezy and listening to him she began to feel better.

In bed she tried to go to sleep quickly. That was the best way, she knew, when something was on your mind. But she could not manage it. She kept on seeing the huge dark shape of Mr Wilberforce outlined against the blue light in the house. The smell still drifted up from the lake. Perhaps it was her imagination that made it seem stronger now. After a while she got up and closed her window. She would sooner be hot she thought than have rotten cabbages in her room. She must have slept then because she came awake with a start. Someone had opened her door.

'Rachel, are you asleep?'

'I was. I'm not now.'

'Sorry,' Theo said. 'Close your eyes.' He turned on the light. 'I've been exploring and I found this book. It's about Auckland's volcanoes. And listen to what it says about the lake. "Lake Pupuke is an explosion crater, containing a fresh water lake. The name for basins of this sort is maar. The lake itself is of extraordinary depth. It lies some 200 metres from the sea and twenty metres above it. An underground drainage system extends through the lava and fresh water can sometimes be seen bubbling through the rocks at Thornes Bay north of Takapuna beach." '

'But it's flat here,' Rachel said.

'Well, evidently you can have flat volcanoes. And we're sitting right on the edge of one. Doesn't it make you feel funny?'

2. THE OLD MAN ON THE MOUNTAIN

At breakfast they both felt heavy and cross. Theo had slept with his windows closed too. Uncle Clarry tried to joke them into better humour.

'Real little lighthouses, aren't they? And both their parents with brown hair. How about that, Noeline? You think there was a red-headed milkman in the street?'

The twins went pale. 'Haven't you ever heard of recessive genes?' Theo asked.

'Blue jeans I've heard of. Not recessive. And I'll tell you something, professor, you use too many big words and your brains'll start coming out your ears.' He gave them ten dollars each 'to paint the town red with'.

They went to their rooms to get ready for the beach. Rachel pulled on her bathing suit in a bad-tempered way. Her aunt and uncle were all right, she decided, but they talked too much. Two weeks of it were going to be hard to take. And ten dollars was far too much money, it seemed like a bribe, even though it was very nice to have. She got her towel and went to Theo's room. He was still in his dressing-gown, standing by his window with a pair of binoculars.

'Where did you get those?'

'They're Uncle Clarry's. Quiet. He's coming out.'

'Who?'

'Mr Wilberforce.'

Rachel looked along the lake shore at the old tree-shaded house. She could see the back porch and steps. Standing there was a man dressed in brown clothes: Mr Wilberforce. As she watched he walked down the steps and vanished behind some trees.

'He looks normal enough,' Theo said. 'Big, that's all.'

'Let me see.'

'Just a minute.'

The man had come into sight again, walking down to the shore. He stood there and stared at the water.

'Theo, can I have a look?'

He handed her the binoculars. She pointed them at Mr Wilberforce, turned the focusing wheel, and the man's face sprang at her. She almost cried out. But it was, as Theo had said, quite a normal face. It was craggy and square. The eyes were set in deep caves, and the hair round the whitish-yellow bald head was grey and spiky.

'What's he doing?' Theo said.

'Reaching into that tree. Theo, he's pulling something off.' She could not see it. The man had something in his hand and was examining it, but his back was towards her. Slowly he turned. She caught a faint gleam of something red-gold against the skin of his palm. She knew at once what it was.

'Theo,' she whispered, 'it's one of my hairs. Remember I got my hair caught in that tree.'

'Are you sure?'

'What else could it be?'

'Here, give me those.' He took the binoculars. 'It's too far to see properly.'

She saw the man's hand move up to his face. 'What's he doing?'

'He seems to be smelling it!'

They watched for a moment longer. Then Rachel said, 'Theo, I think . . .' She stopped. It seemed foolish.

'What?'

'Suppose the smell in the lake comes from them. And they can smell us . . .'

'How could it come from them?'

'I don't know.'

'If you're right I hope we smell a bit better.' He grinned at her but she was too worried to laugh. She took the binoculars back. Yes, the man was sniffing, there was no mistake about that. Suddenly he looked up. He looked straight at her. His eyes fastened on hers down the binoculars. They were still as puddles, a grey stony colour. She gave a cry and jumped behind the curtain.

'Theo, he saw me.'

Theo was hiding too, peering out. 'It's all right, he's going.'

The man walked up the lawn, vanished behind the trees, reappeared and climbed the steps. Mrs Wilberforce met him on the porch. He showed her Rachel's hair, held it close to her nose. They both stared at Uncle Clarry's house. The twins hid. When they looked out again the old people had gone.

'Theo, we'll have to tell someone.'

'Tell them what? It's too crazy.'

'Who do you think they are?'

'Just looneys.'

'It's more than that.'

He said nothing; but she saw he agreed.

'The woman, she was so tiny. She only came to his chest.'

'It's just that he's so big,' Theo said. 'We'd better keep well away from there.'

They spent the rest of the morning on the beach. The noise of motor-boats heading out of the ski-lane made it difficult for them to hear each other. But soon they forgot the Wilberforces. Theo watched the boats with fascination. Some of them went so fast they bounced on the surface. Their engines sounded like aeroplanes. Rachel spent most of her time in the water. She floated and practised her backstroke and watched ships go by in the channel. They looked like toys outlined against Rangitoto. She wondered why she had found the island frightening. Today, in sunlight, it was a colour between blue and green and it almost seemed to float. Its peaks, 200 metres above the sea, were so neat and even they might have been modelled by a sculptor.

Lunch-time came. They started for home round the reef. 'We can look for the fresh-water springs at Thornes Bay,' Theo said.

They hunted in the broken rocks on the water-line, climbing into crevices and under ledges. Several times Theo tasted water lying in rock pools, but it was always salt. 'Maybe the fresh stuff only comes in winter.' They climbed up to the road and set off for home.

As they climbed, an old man who had been sitting on the sand at the end of the beach rose to his feet and watched them. He was a thin old man, with skin browned by the sun and eyes of unfaded blue. He was dressed in sandals and shorts and a red shirt and an orange hat made of towelling. Most old men would have looked odd in such clothes, but they suited him. He looked as if he had spent his life in the sun.

He had been close to the children all through the morning. He had watched them swimming and sunbathing, followed them round the reef, listened to their talk, often from no more than a few metres away. But they had not seen him. He was clever at not being seen. When they had climbed the steps at Thornes Bay and gone out of sight up the road, he turned and made his way back round the reef to Takapuna. He smiled as he walked – a smile more sad than happy.

'Yes,' he murmured, 'Rachel and Theo Matheson.'

He walked through the streets of the town and came to a

little house behind a high hedge. In the kitchen he crossed to the window, where two white objects lay on the sill. They were not what they seemed. Only he knew what they were. He laid his hands on them, felt their warmth.

'I must get you ready,' he whispered. 'The ones who can use you have come.'

In the afternoon Aunt Noeline took Rachel and Theo on a sight-seeing tour. Ricky, grumbling, acted as chauffeur. They were in his mother's Mini and she would not let him drive fast. They went over the bridge, round the waterfront drive, through the Domain. But when they stopped outside the Museum Theo said, 'If you don't mind, Aunt Noeline, I'd rather go to the top of Mount Eden.'

'Me too,' Rachel said.

'That's an idea,' Ricky said. 'Who wants to look at stuffed fish?'

Aunt Noeline gave a sigh, but agreed. So they drove to Mount Eden and Ricky enjoyed himself scooting the Mini up the hillside road. Standing on the summit was like standing on the edge of a cliff. The whole of western and southern Auckland lay at their feet. They saw streets with tiny cars on them; and parks, race-courses, hospitals, schools. The Manukau Harbour was like a lake inside the coastal hills. Here and there volcanic cones broke above the trees and the roofs of houses.

'That's One Tree Hill,' Ricky said, pointing to a steep cone with a single tree and a monument on top. 'And that big one over there is Mount Wellington.'

They climbed to the viewing platform below the trig point and the other half of the city came into sight. 'There are the wharves and the bridge at Rangitoto. You can't see our place.'

'I can see the lake,' Rachel said. 'See, Theo. It's just a tiny silver line.'

But both children were more interested in the crater. It was a hundred metres across and perfectly shaped as a porridge bowl. Grass grew down its sides and over the bottom. It was hard to imagine it blowing out lava. But Rachel wondered how scientists really knew when a volcano was extinct. Perhaps this one was just sleeping – having a sleep of a hundred thousand years. One day it would wake up and destroy the city. She was going to ask Theo what he thought of that, though she supposed he would make fun of her, when a strange prickling feeling came in her head. It was like pins-and-needles. She gave a little cry; then was quiet, for a voice had begun to say words. At first they were furry, coming through a sound like radio static, coming it seemed from a very long way off. Then they grew stronger, and she made them out. It was someone saying deep inside her head, 'Rachel, Theo, do not be afraid.'

'I'm not afraid,' she whispered.

Theo's voice came from her left, 'Rachel?'

'Yes, I heard it.'

'Look, Rachel.' He was pointing over the crater. An old man was standing in the pine trees on the rim. His red shirt showed like fire. Even from this distance they felt his eyes looking into them.

'Was it him talking to us?'

'It must have been.'

'How did he do it?'

'I don't know. Rachel – it must be *him*.'

'Yes. Yes. Of course.'

They had not forgotten. Now they lived it again. They knew the terror of being lost; they lay in the damp icy ferns; they slept, and had wonderful dreams, and woke warm, and an old man smiled down at them, and told them to remember. They remembered. For eight years it had lain in their minds, and though they had given up speaking of it – people only laughed – they had always known the man, their friend, would come back. He had said one day they would know who he was. Now, though they could not see his face, they knew that this was him.

'He must have brought us up here.'

'Yes. I didn't want to come, did you? I just heard myself saying it.'

'Come on.'

Ricky was back at the viewing platform and Aunt Noeline in the car reading a magazine. The twins glanced at them, then set off for the other side of the crater. They went along the rim, clambering like goats. The old man watched them coming. For a moment they lost sight of him as they went through a clump of pine trees. Then they ran along a grassy flat to the place where they had seen him. But when they arrived they gave a cry of disappointment. The old man was gone. They peered into the trees and down the grassy slopes that fell to the city. Nowhere. He was gone. And again the pins-and-needles came in their minds. The voice said, 'Look at this mountain. Look at it well. And at Rangitoto.'

'Why?' Theo whispered.

'They are the poles.'

'Did you bring us here?'

'Yes. But look at them.'

'What do you mean, poles?'

'Look at them. You must come here again.'

So they looked across the city and the sea at Rangitoto, and looked into the crater at Mount Eden. The places were ordinary enough, perhaps a little dark, a little threatening, but that, they thought, was because clouds had come up from the south and hidden the sun. After a while Theo said, 'Are you still there?'

'Yes.'

'How do you do this?'

'I'll tell you one day.'

'Will we meet you?'

'Soon.'

There was quiet. 'Thank you for saving us,' Rachel said.

'Thank you for being what you are. And now, children, go back to your car. Your aunt will start to worry soon.'

They turned to go back. And they saw the old man on the rim they had come from, standing against the sky. They ran again, through the trees, over the flat, along the broken ground on the crater rim. When they reached the cars he had vanished again. They ran across the parking lot and looked down the mountain side, but saw only grazing cattle. 'How does he do it?' They clambered into the Mini, red-faced and breathless. Aunt Noeline put down her magazine.

'What energetic children.'

'Did you see him?'

'Who?'

'That old man.'

'My dears, I've been reading . . .'

Ricky got in the car.

'Did you see him, Ricky?'

'An old man in a red shirt.'

'He was over the other side and then he came round here.'

'I saw him,' Ricky said. 'That was old Jonesy.'

'Who?'

'Old Jonesy. Mr Jones. The bloke I was telling you about. He hangs around the Wilberforces' place. Wonder what he was doing over here.'

'He was the one who saved us when we were lost.'

'Now, children,' Aunt Noeline said, 'that was just fantasy.'

They said no more, were sorry in fact that they had said so much. Ricky drove down the winding road on the side of the mountain. Aunt Noeline smiled. 'I wouldn't worry, dears. Mr Jones may be a bit odd but he's very kind. Ricky, keep your speed down . . . And I've got just a tiny suspicion this is one of your games.'

'What games?'

'Those ones you used to play when you were smaller. Finding things.'

They blushed. There had been a time when they had been able to send messages to each other – telepathy, their father had called it. Their favourite trick had been for one of them to hide something in a room and then with closed eyes concentrate on the object, sending its picture to the other, who would walk in and go straight to it – an ear-ring or marble or paper-weight in some unlikely place. But they had given that up. It was part of their 'twinship', which they were anxious to drop. They wanted to be themselves. So they sat quiet on the drive home. The old man – Mr Jones – was not a game. They were certain of that. He was the one who had saved them. And turning their minds back to that time, to their night in the bush, their dreaming comfortable sleep, and their happy waking, they remembered, for the first time in eight years, that he had spoken of a task he would call them to do. Now he had shown them the mountains – Rangitoto, Mount Eden. So the task was there. At the poles. Theo puzzled about the word. Poles were things that were opposite, but joined. He could not work it out. At the other end of the seat, Rachel watched Rangitoto. As they drove up the harbour bridge the island seemed to climb up from the sea. She felt cold.

In Takapuna she asked to be let down. She made the excuse of wanting to go to the library. The truth was she wanted to be by herself to think things out.

Theo said, 'I'm going to have a canoe ride on the lake. Get me a book though.'

'And me,' Aunt Noeline cried. 'Here's my card. A nice murder. Not too gruesome.'

The library was down a street towards the beach. For a

while she wandered about, trying to make sense of the things that had happened. But it all seemed part of a dream. In this bright place, full of people and books, with happy-looking girls behind the desk, it seemed impossible that any of it could really have happened. A voice inside her head, an old man who vanished, a task that must be done – and the smell of the lake, people who sniffed at hairs. Impossible. And yet – Mr Jones had saved them, he had been there in the bush eight years ago. She was certain of that.

Rachel sighed. It was too difficult. She hoped that soon he would come and explain. In the meantime, it was nearly closing time. She must get some books. She chose two for herself and two for Theo. Then she hurried to the rental shelves and started pulling out murder mysteries. Their covers made them all seem horrible. What was a 'nice' murder? But at last she found one that seemed as if it would do. It was called *Lost in the Lake* and its cover showed a stretch of dark water with a twisted hand coming out of it. At least there was no blood.

She pushed the other books back into the shelves. One slipped out and fell on the floor. She bent down to pick it up, pushing her arm round the base of the shelves. But as her fingers closed on it she felt something grip her. She gave a small cry of surprise. A hand had taken her arm, a long, old, very brown hand; and she made no move to get away, for the touch was warm and not in the least alarming. She stood up and looked into the eyes of the old man in the red shirt – Mr Jones. He was watching her with friendliness and sadness. She knew she had nothing to fear. The warmth of his touch was creeping up her arm. It was almost as if she were lowering it slowly into a bath of warm water. He kept his grip, firm and light, and seemed to be listening. She knew she was being tested, some message was passing through her skin to his hand. She longed for it to be the right one and she kept very still.

At last he smiled. 'Don't be frightened, Rachel.'

'I'm not frightened.'

He let go her wrist and turned away. In a moment she saw him go out the door and walk away down the street. She took her books to the desk and had them issued. Then she walked home. The warmth in her arm grew stronger. By the time she reached the lake it had crept through the whole of her body.

Theo was in his room, sitting on his bed and staring at his hands with an odd excited look.

'Rachel, you'll never guess what's happened.'

'I want to tell you what happened to me. The old man –'

'No, me first. I went across to the other side of the lake and when I got out of the canoe to look at the yachts the old man was there.'

She knew exactly what he was going to say.

'He came up and took hold of my wrist. As if he was taking my pulse. Right here. And then he just looked at me for a while. And he said, "Don't be frightened, Theo." And the funny thing was, I wasn't. I'm not.'

'What time was it?'

'About twenty minutes ago. Five o'clock.'

'That's when he was with me in the library. Within a few minutes anyway.'

'Rachel, that's teleportation. You know, moving yourself with thought.'

'What about the warmth? Have you got that?'

'Yes. It's right through me. But I don't feel hot. I mean sweaty. It's different from that. Wait on.' He hurried out of the room and came back with a thermometer. 'I found this in the bathroom. Open your mouth.'

They took Rachel's temperature first, then Theo's. Both were normal – thirty-seven degrees.

'But I feel about fifty-five degrees.'

'Me too. But listen Rachel, he told me to stay off the lake.'

'Why?'

'I don't know. All he said was, "Never go on the lake. Tell your sister." I had to pull the canoe back round the shore. It must be because of – them.' He nodded out the window.

'The Wilberforces?'

'Have you noticed the smell? You can tell it comes from there.'

They looked at the Wilberforces' house and for a moment felt colder. But then they sat on the bed and the warmth returned.

'What do we do?'

'Wait for him to get in touch with us.'

'I hope he's not too long. There are a lot of questions I want to ask.'

'Like, who is he?'

'What is he?'

'Yes,' Theo agreed. 'And what are the Wilberforces?'

3. THE STONES

They slept with their windows closed to keep out the smell. The warmth stayed in their bodies but somehow gave them the temperature they required. Their sleep was as deep and comfortable as any they had known, although once in the night Rachel dreamed she heard a slithering sound outside her window and a coughing like a cat trying to be sick. But it lasted only a moment and after that she slept as soundly as before.

After breakfast they stayed around the house. They agreed they should wait for the old man to get in touch with them. Halfway through the morning Uncle Clarry called them outside.

'There's a funny sort of dust all over the grass. I've never seen anything like it. It's like flour but it's sort of sticky and grey. Have you kids been touching something you shouldn't?'

'No, Uncle.'

'It's under your windows. It even goes a couple of feet up the walls. Are you sure you didn't throw something out?'

'No.'

'I wonder if Ricky's been messing with something.'

The twins touched the dust with their fingers. It had an unpleasant feeling and clung to their skin. And it carried a trace of the rotten cabbage smell. Uncle Clarry did not notice that.

Later in the morning they went up to Rachel's room and looked at the Wilberforces' house. They studied it through Uncle Clarry's binoculars. Some of the windows were painted over and others had blinds drawn down to the sills. The roof-iron was rusty and the fancy woodwork under the eaves was rotting away. Broken down-pipes crawled down the walls like snakes. Nothing moved. And nothing stirred outside. There seemed to be no birds in the trees or hedges.

The postman came up the street. He passed the Wilberforces' box without a glance. But as he went by the stone fence and the padlocked iron gate, one of the blinds in the house seemed to tremble. The twins shivered.

'I wish Mr Jones would come,' Rachel said.

They took their library books and went down to the living-room. It was warm down there.

After lunch Ricky found them sitting on the sofa.

'What's the matter with you kids?'

'Nothing.'

'Well, get outside. The sun's shining.'

'I got sunburned yesterday.'

'Me too.'

'Put some cream on then. Come on. You both look as if you're missing Mummy.'

'Cut it out, Ricky.'

'Tell you what. I'm not doing anything. We'll go for a spin in the boat.'

'Hey, that'd be great.'

'Get into your togs then. We'll go out to Rangitoto.'

He hooked the boat to the buggy while they were changing. They climbed in beside him and he drove up the right-of-way on to the road. Theo and Rachel looked back towards the Wilberforces'. The iron gates of the old house were open. A huge black car nosed out like an eel from a hole and set off after them.

38

'Ricky, have you seen that car before?'

He looked in his rear-vision mirror. 'Yeah. It belongs to those weirdos up the street. Converted hearse. They probably keep bodies in it.' He laughed.

The car followed them all the way to the beach, keeping well behind. But as Ricky was backing down the boat-ramp it turned about and drove away up the hill towards the main road.

'Maybe they're watching to see we don't meet Mr Jones,' Theo whispered. 'Can you see him?'

They searched the beach with their eyes until Ricky yelled at them to give him a hand. 'What a dozy pair. I can't launch this thing by myself. Hold it while I get the buggy parked.'

Soon he was back and they climbed into the boat and set off along the edge of the reef towards the open sea. The day was calm and the *Sea Lady* sped along as Ricky opened her up. She drummed on the water, scarcely touching the swells, and the twins forgot the Wilberforces in their excitement. The spray flew back and wet their faces.

'We're wide open now. Want to drive?'

They took turns, curving the boat in wide sweeps, but always straightening her up towards Rangitoto. They closed on the island at a startling rate. The twins hadn't realized it was so close.

'How far is it from the beach, Ricky?'

'About ten kilometres. We can do it in quarter of an hour.'

The coastline behind them had flattened out. They picked out the beaches – Takapuna, Cheltenham, Narrow Neck – with cliffs between them. The houses were tiny boxes clustered together and the trees no taller than grass. But it was the island that held their attention. It seemed to grow taller and bend over them. It was much larger than they had thought and the bush was thicker and wilder. A walk to the peak would take hours.

Suddenly Rachel did not like it. She did not like its black rocks or the colour of its bush.

'I don't want to go ashore, Ricky.'

'I wasn't going to. We'll just cruise in by the lighthouse and then head round towards the Noises.'

'We should have brought fishing lines,' Theo said.

Ricky shook his head. 'There's nothing here. Something seems to have scared them away.'

When they were a hundred metres from shore Ricky took the wheel. He dropped the boat's speed and they went in close to the lighthouse. Yachts and run-abouts were dotted over the channel. An oil tanker, low in the water, was picking up its pilot. Close to the island the *Sea Lady* was far from them all.

Rachel moved close to Theo. 'Can you smell it?'

'Just a whiff.'

'That means they come out here.'

The rocks on the water's edge were broken and jagged but here and there were patches of sand. Ricky took the boat in close and crawled her along almost touching the black lava. For ten minutes they made their way north along the shoreline. High above them the mountain lost its shape. The sky clouded over and the bush turned the colour of mud. Out in the channel the tanker let out three sounds like the roaring of a bull. Rachel shivered.

'I'm getting cold, Ricky. Can we go back?'

'We've just got out here.'

'I think it's going to rain.'

But Ricky was staring behind her. 'Porpoises. Look.'

Back in the direction of the lighthouse three grey shapes were cruising towards them with their fins breaking the water.

'You don't often see that,' Ricky said.

Theo was peering closely at the fish. Suddenly his eye caught a movement deep in the water. Something was surfacing fast towards the boat.

'They aren't porpoises,' he cried, 'they're sharks.'

He lunged past Ricky and pulled the throttle open. The boat stood up on its stern, then jerked away at a speed that had them clutching the sides to keep their feet. It careered wildly until Ricky grabbed the wheel. He straightened her up. A huge black shape broke the surface on their left and leaped high in the air. It twisted in its flight, lashing at the boat with its tail, then fell back with a splash that threw water across the cabin.

'He tried to ram us,' Ricky shouted. The boat jolted sideways, nearly throwing Theo out. Another shark had struck a blow on its side.

'Down. Lie in the bottom.' Ricky had the throttle wide open and he drove the boat on a zig-zag course. The two sharks dived for another attack. But the Sea Lady was at her top speed and in a moment they appeared again twenty metres behind. The others were even further back.

'We're losing them,' Ricky yelled. He had the boat headed for Takapuna. In a moment he called the twins up to the middle. 'She'll run better with the weight here. Keep your eye open for leaks. That was one hell of a bang she took.'

'Sharks don't attack like that,' Theo said.

'These ones did. It's lucky they weren't real big ones. That first bloke that had a go at us was only about a couple of metres. Still, if he'd hit us square on he would have smashed a hole.'

'It wasn't just anyone they were after,' Rachel said – but Theo gave her a look and she kept quiet.

In ten minutes they were back at the ramp. Ricky went for the buggy while the twins held the boat in the shallow water. The sharks had dropped from sight not far from Rangitoto.

'This is getting serious,' Theo said.

'I could smell them, Theo.'

'So could I.'

'All I want is to get my feet out of the water.'

They helped Ricky haul the boat on the trailer. A grey mark like a bruise ran up its side. Ricky went pale when he saw it. 'Talk about lucky. If you hadn't seen them when you did, Theo, we'd be dead.'

He drove up the ramp and set off up the hill. The twins sat close together, wrapped in their towels. In spite of the warmth still in them from the old man's touch they were feeling chilled. They kept a lookout for the hearse, but the streets were full of camper-vans and cars pulling caravans. Ricky stopped at the corner to let traffic go by on the main road. It was Rachel who saw Mr Jones first. She felt her head drawn round by a force like magnetism. He was standing on the footpath by the hotel. Today his shirt was blue. He smiled at her. Theo felt the same force. They forgot the sharks. 'Rachel, Theo, come with me,' his voice said in their minds. At once they climbed out of the buggy.

'Hey, where are you going?' Ricky yelled. Then cars behind him sounded their horns and he had to drive away.

'Tell Auntie we'll buy a pie for lunch,' Theo yelled after him.

Mr Jones had crossed the road and was walking up a footpath that led to the lake. Some way up he stopped and waited for them. They crossed and followed him, always a dozen metres behind, as though this were an instruction. They turned a corner and went along a street of houses built in brick and tile. They had concrete or wrought-iron fences and plaster seals with bird-baths on their noses. But halfway along was a high green hedge with a red iron roof behind it. The old man opened the gate and went in. The house was a white cottage with flowers growing wild over its lawns.

The twins stopped at the gate. 'Remember what Mum always says about strangers?'

'He isn't a stranger. He saved us. Besides, Aunt Noeline knows him.'

They went up the path without fear and through the door Mr Jones held open for them. They found themselves in a kitchen that also seemed to serve as a living-room. It contained a sofa and an easy chair as well as a table and stove and fridge.

'Welcome, children.'

He spoke normally. 'I'm glad we can meet properly at last.'

He took them to the sofa and sat them down. Then he lowered himself into the chair. 'I'm sorry I've been so long.' His face was older than it had been when he had saved them, even older, it seemed, than it had been in the library and by the lake.

Rachel smiled at him. 'You look tired.'

'I am, young lady.'

'We'll make you a cup of tea.'

'A good idea. You have one too. Then we can talk.'

She went to the cupboards and found the things she needed.

Theo put the kettle on. He came back to the sofa. 'How do you talk in our minds? Is it telepathy?'

'That's one word for it. We simply call it speaking.'

'Can you teach us to do it?'

'I think so.'

'From far away?'

'Ah no. I can do that, although it drains me of strength. But you and your sister will have to be able to see each other.'

'So we have to have a connection. It'll be like the telephone, not like radio.'

Mr Jones laughed. He looked pleased. 'You think things out. You're the practical one. And your sister's the dreamer.'

'Is that why you're interested in us?'

'More than that. Much more.'

'Are you looking into our minds now?'

'I only peek when I have to, Theo.'

'You can do other things too.'

'What sort of things?'

'Well, teleportation. Like when you got from the library to the lake. And when you got away from us on the mountain. Can you teach us that too?'

'No. Not that.'

Theo frowned. 'It would have been fun. Have you been watching us since we were babies?'

'Since I found you in the bush. But here's Rachel. You found a tray, my dear? And some biscuits?'

'The kettle hasn't boiled yet. I'll get the tea in a minute.' She looked at the old man carefully. She felt very close to him, and reminded herself that after all she had known him for eight years. 'Why are you sad?'

'Can you see that?'

'Yes. I think so. You're very sad. Sadder than anyone I've ever known. I think someone you loved must have died.'

'Yes, that's so. Someone. Long ago. I didn't think you would see it. Now tell me what you notice about this room.'

She looked about her. 'It's warm. It's got a comfortable feeling. But – it's a sad room. Both the pictures are sunsets.'

'Yes.' The old man laughed. 'You're very good, Rachel. You have the gift.'

'Was that part of a test?'

'A small part.'

'Can you tell us how we got warm when you touched us. We're still warm.'

'Oh, that's just an idea I put in your minds. But now, my dear, the kettle seems to be boiling.'

They drank tea and ate biscuits. When they had cleared everything away, the twins sat and watched Mr Jones.

Rachel thought he was very ordinary looking, just an old man with grey hair and a stubbly chin and bony hands. Most old men were like that. But there were lines on his face that seemed to mark some tragedy, something too deep to be spoken of. She felt sorry for him and she sat with folded hands, waiting for him to begin.

Theo was more impatient. 'You said there was a job we had to do.'

'Ah, you remember. Yes, there is a job. A dangerous job.'

'We don't mind,' Rachel said.

'Think, Rachel. Think before you speak. Very dangerous. You may lose your lives.'

They were silent.

'But you are the only ones,' Mr Jones said.

'Is it – important?'

'*Yes*.' The word was spoken silently in their minds, and they knew beyond any question it was true.

'We'll do it.'

And Theo said, 'Is it to do with the Wilberforces?'

Mr Jones bent close. His eyes seemed to bore into them. 'What do you know of the Wilberforces?'

'Nothing. But . . . Ricky – our cousin – he said he's seen you hanging round their place.'

'Has he? Well, I watch them . . . But it's too soon yet for you to think about Wilberforces. Don't get close to them, that's all. Don't let them scent you. And stay off the lake. Never go on the lake.'

'We won't,' they breathed. They were too frightened to tell him Mr Wilberforce had one of Rachel's hairs.

'But now, my dears, put them out of your minds. They will not harm you. They think I can only use identical twins. They have no way of knowing I found you when you were babies, and taught you many things. Yes, without your knowing. Now let's get on to more pleasant things. I must teach you to speak.'

'Speak?' Rachel asked.

'What you call telepathy.'

'Do we sort of think what we want to say?'

'Nothing so simple, Theo. You use a little poetry.'

'Poetry?'

'We'll start with you. Are you ready?'

'Yes.'

'Then make your mind clear. Push everything out of it. Not a single thought left. Your mind is a pool of water, very clear, absolutely still. Now Rachel is going to drop some pebbles in. Concentrate on that with all your mind. And forget me, forget my voice. Rachel, this isn't hypnotism. I'm not making him deaf, he is making himself. He can't hear me now. His mind is a pool of water.'

Theo sat with a faint smile on his face. He saw nothing, heard nothing. He waited for pebbles to drop.

'Now, Rachel, your mind must be cleaned out too. Get all that rubbish out. Decide what you want to tell your brother. Have you decided? Now turn each word into a little pebble. What colour do you want them? White? Now hold them, my dear, hold them in your hand. I'm going to leave it to you now. When you are ready, when you have them – are they warm? – just drop them one by one into the pool . . .'

She held the words in her hand. They were white as ivory and warm as blood. She dropped them one by one . . . and Theo felt them sink into his mind and turn as they settled. 'Theo, I'm not the least bit scared, are you?'

'No,' he said, and the word made him wince with pain. He had not expected sound.

'Theo, you can speak as well as hear,' Mr Jones said.

It took them little more than half an hour before they were able to do it perfectly. Each could 'speak' and 'listen'. Soon they were able to do it without the image of pebble and pool. They simply dropped words into each other's minds – although Rachel named the process 'pebbling'. Then they found they could 'pebble' with Mr Jones, and to two minds at once. For another half hour they sat holding a soundless conversation – smiling, frowning, looking earnest. It was tiring at first, and each of the twins, resting for a short while outside the 'talk', had a moment of panic at the weirdness of it. But quickly they were drawn back in and then it seemed the most natural form of speech and the use of the tongue, the making of sounds, clumsy and primitive.

'Can anyone do this?' Rachel asked.

'No. Just a few. Just a few of your race.'

'Why can we? And why is it so easy?'

'It's easy because it's not a skill, it doesn't have to be learnt. The ability has always been in you and Theo. It was simply waiting for you to discover it – like a new land in a strange sea.'

'Is it because we're twins?' Theo asked.

'Yes. Because you're bonded. Your minds work together. But it's also because you're different from each other – a sort of north pole and a south. Theo, you're practical – you like to know why and how – and Rachel, you're intuitive. You understand without knowing the reasons. But also it's because you have red hair. That gives you special qualities.'

'Have you taught other people to pebble?'

'I've tried. For many years I've hunted for a pair. But some have gone only a little way and then grown scared – and one . . .'

His face grew dark with sadness and the twins trying to send words through found them bouncing back. It was like being struck with fists.

'I'm sorry, my dears. That was stupid of me – and cruel. But it still makes me sad, you see. They were twins, like you. But identical. Two boys. And they learned as quickly as you. They had red hair. They were amazing children. They were brave and clever and quick – and I grew to love them so much that I became careless. I forgot to watch – to remember I was watched . . .'

'What happened?'

'They died.'

Rachel felt herself almost in tears. 'How?'

'I can't tell you. Not yet. I will one day.'

'Was it long ago?'

'A very long time. Many many years.'

Theo sat with his head bowed. Suddenly he looked up. 'It's going to be dangerous for us too, isn't it?'

'Yes, Theo. I told you that.'

'There's something you want us to do. You wanted those others to do it and they got killed. Isn't that right?'

'Yes Theo, it's right.'

'What is it then? I think it's time we knew.'

The old man looked at them for a moment. They did not try to send any words to him. The deep withdrawn look on his face told them his mind was closed. Then he sighed – the first sound in the room for many moments – and stood up.

'I want you to learn to use these.' He walked across the room and took something from the window-sill over the sink. He came back to the twins and held them out, one on the palm of each hand: two stones. In size they were somewhere between a golf ball and a tennis ball, but flattened slightly. They were river-bed pebbles, Theo thought, and not especially good ones – smooth enough but without any life in their colour. It was simply white, flat white, like milk, although one had a faint tinge of grey.

'What are they?'

Mr Jones made no answer. He placed one pebble on the palm of Rachel's hand and the other on Theo's. They were warm from the sun which had been shining on the sill, and heavier than the twins had expected.

'These are what took me so long. I had to get them ready again. It's years since anyone tried to use them.'

'They're just stones,' Theo said.

'Not just stones. *The* stones.'

Theo did not care for mysteries. 'Yes, but what are they for? I mean, they must be special the way you're talking about them. Are they magic?'

'They're a weapon,' Rachel said. Her face had gone pale.

'I can't tell you, Rachel. You must see them first. And so far you can't. I didn't expect you to. It's possible you may never be able to.'

'What do you mean "see"?' Theo persisted.

'They aren't what they seem. But I can't tell you what they are or how to use them.'

'What do we do, then?'

'Slow down, Theo. Take it slowly. You've got to see the stones the way they are. The only way to do that is to take them into your mind. Make your mind a pool of water again and drop the stone in gently. No splash. This one's yours. Turn it round, look at it. You too, Rachel – this one here. Don't be frightened. It won't hurt you.'

They tried. They looked at the stones from every angle, let them float like balloons and settle gently, spun them, turned them, peered at them closely, into their grain, as though through a microscope. Theo even tried to break his in half. But they remained heavy, white, dull, flat, impenetrable – stones.

'I'm sorry . . .' Theo said.

'Me too.'

'They're just . . .' He shrugged.

'Do you see nothing? In the shape? The colour? Try again.'

But it was no good. When the twins looked at the old man again he looked tired, sick. His face had fallen into lines of pain and age.

'We're sorry, Mr Jones. If you could give us a clue . . .'

'No. I should have known . . . It's no good. They have

won. You need to be identical twins.' He looked at them angrily. 'Why aren't you identical?'

For a long time there was silence. Theo and Rachel stared at the stones hopelessly. Mr Jones had closed his eyes. At last he smiled. 'I'm sorry. It isn't your fault. I must let you go now.'

'Isn't there anything we can do?'

'Forget. That's all. I must apologize for what I'm going to do. But it will be better if you forget this afternoon. I'll give you some new memories – an afternoon on the beach. Will that be all right?'

'No. You mustn't.'

'It will be better, Rachel.'

'But just because of a pair of stupid old stones. I mean, they're exactly the same, just old white pebbles.'

'Nearly the same,' Theo said.

'Oh, stop being like a schoolteacher. Can't you see what he's going to do?'

'I know. But they're not exactly the same. It's not important, but my one's a little bit grey.'

The old man had caught his breath. For a moment it seemed he was about to break in, then he drew back and let them carry on.

'It isn't. You're making it up just because you think he wants to hear something. It's white. Dead white. Like paper. My one's the one that's different.'

'Phooey. How?'

'Can't you see, it's got a little bit of brown in it. Just a tinge. But it's something. Not just stupid old white.'

'Stop,' a voice said quietly in their heads.

They looked at Mr Jones guiltily. His face was very calm and no longer old. 'What else do you see? You, Theo?'

'Nothing else. Just a bit of grey – I mean, off-white. Like paint that's had a drop of blue put in.'

'Blue. Rachel?'

'I don't see it. But mine's got a tiny bit of brown – almost gold.'

'Anything else? Look closely.'

They looked but there was nothing.

'It's heavy,' Theo said. 'Heavier than it should be. Not like lead though. Lighter than that.'

'Rachel?'

'Yes. And it's still warm. I mean, a stone shouldn't stay warm that long should it? Twenty minutes?'

'Rachel, these stones don't feel the sun. Or the cold. They are always the same.'

'They were warm when you gave them to us. Weren't they, Theo?'

'A bit.'

'That means they recognized you.'

'Recognized? Stones?'

Mr Jones shook his head. 'No. You've had enough for today. You've come very far. Much farther than I had any right to hope. I'm going to do something now that you won't like. Give me the stones.'

Reluctantly they handed them over. He put them back on the window-sill.

'If they're so important you shouldn't leave them there,' Theo said.

The old man smiled. 'They're safe, Theo. And I like to remind certain prowlers I have that they exist.'

'Who?'

'Tomorrow. You must learn more about the stones first. Now take them into your minds. Have you done that? I'm going to lock them there and when you come back tomorrow you'll know a good deal more about them. But I have to stop you poking at them and wondering what they are. So I'm going to make you forget. I'll give you the memory of an afternoon on the beach. You won't remember this visit till I call you tomorrow.'

'No –'

'Yes, Rachel. It's necessary.'

'Will we be able to pebble?'

'No. I'm sorry. Not until I clear your minds again.'

'But can't you tell us now what it's about? I don't think it's fair –'

'Very few things are fair, Theo. And tomorrow I'll tell you everything. I promise. Now are you ready?'

'But –' He was going to ask what the creatures were that had attacked the *Sea Lady*. But Mr Jones raised his hand and he found he could not speak, either with his voice or with his mind.

'I'm sorry, Theo. I must do what has to be done. Now, do you have the stone in your mind? Hard and clear?'

'Yes.' He was able to say that.

'You, Rachel?'

'Yes.'

'Goodbye, my dears. Sleep well. You are very special people. You are the hope of your race.'

They were walking along the road towards home. The sun was low in the sky and a cool wind had sprung up from the sea. They shivered and wrapped their towels around their shoulders.

'Are we late?' Rachel asked.

Theo looked at his watch. 'It's nearly six. We'd better run. Auntie'll be mad.'

They began to jog.

After a while Theo said, 'It's funny Mr Jones didn't get in touch.'

'I've been thinking about that too.'

'Are you still warm from yesterday?'

'Yes. Not as much though.'

'I can still smell the lake.'

'So can I.'

'Do you think Mr Jones can smell it?'

'I don't know, but I wish he'd come.'

Theo was quiet for a time. 'Maybe,' he said, 'maybe he put us through a test yesterday. Holding our hands like that. And maybe he discovered we were no good.'

'Yes,' Rachel said, 'that's what I've been thinking.'

It made them unhappy.

4. THINGS THAT GO QUACK IN THE NIGHT

Rachel was sleeping fitfully, dreaming of fish and rubies and fires that licked round her face without burning, when her door opened and Theo came in. She woke at once and sat up.

'Have you been having dreams too?'

'Nightmares,' he said. 'About those things that chased us. Listen, Rachel, there's something wrong. We spent the whole afternoon on the beach and I even swam out to that big yacht. But I didn't think about the sharks once.'

'I didn't see you swim out,' she said. 'We spent all the time lying in the sun – and my sunburn's no worse than before.'

Theo sat down. 'Someone's fooling round with our minds.'

'Who? Mr Jones?'

'It's got to be. If he doesn't come tomorrow we've got to ask Auntie where he lives. We can't just sit here.'

She saw he had Uncle Clarry's binoculars round his neck. 'What are you doing with those?'

'Watching the Wilberforces' house. I thought I might see Mr Jones.'

'Did you see anything?'

'Only the man. He was standing on the lawn. The door's open. Have a look.'

He handed her the binoculars. The lake was lit by the moon shining from behind Uncle Clarry's house. The Wilberforces' lawn was silver, with black tree-shadows slanting across it. The house lay deep in shadow, but when she had focused the binoculars she saw the cave of the porch.

'You can't tell if the door's open or not.'

'I haven't heard it close. The slightest sound carries. I heard a noise like ducks quacking a while back. And a sort of coughing.'

'Coughing?' She remembered the dream she had had the night before. But before she could tell him about it she felt a prickling in her mind, the pins-and-needles again. She had turned away from the Wilberforces' house, but felt her eyes drawn back to it. A voice whispered hoarsely in her head, 'Help me. Please help me.'

'Theo.'

'I heard it.'

'Help me, twins. Before it is too late.'

'It must be Mr Jones.'

'Quiet.'

'Help me. He-elp.' The voice faded away, died with an echo.

'It came from over there. They must have him prisoner.'

'Unless it's a trick.'

'But he's the only one who can talk to us like that. Remember Mount Eden.'

Suddenly the voice was back. It gave a long agonized cry that made them clutch their heads with pain. 'He-elp.'

'Oh, Theo, it's got to be him.'

'Yes.'

'What shall we do?'

'We've got to go over there.'

'No –'

'There's no other way. He saved us, remember.'

'We could tell Uncle Clarry.'

'He'd think we were mad.'

That was true. She shivered. 'What's the time?'

'Half past two.'

'How will we get there?'

'In the canoe.'

'But he said not to go on the lake.'

'It's the quickest way. And the quietest. We'll take the torch from Uncle Clarry's car. And my camera.'

'Why the camera?'

'We might get some shots of something. For the police. We can use the paddles for clubs. If we have to.'

They dressed. Soon they had the canoe on the water. Theo worked it silently along the band of shadow by the shore-line. Rachel sat in the bow holding the camera and torch. No sound or movement broke the stillness of the lake. Several cars went by on the road to Milford but they seemed in another world. Rachel felt the rushes brush her arm. Three houses slipped behind them. She kept her eyes on the jutting piece of land where the Wilberforces' lawn met the water. The smell was very strong. She was sure the Wilberforces were somewhere in the night.

Theo nosed the canoe into the reeds beyond the vacant section. A faint bluish light showed in the Wilberforces' porch.

'That means the door's still open. Quiet.' He heard the creaking sound of something heavy moving on floor boards. A dark shape came down the steps with a smaller one behind.

'It's both of them. Keep as still as you can.'

The Wilberforces moved down the lawn, keeping in the shade of trees. They stopped out of the twins' sight. One, two, three minutes passed. A single cough sounded, a single quack.

'What are they doing?'

'Shsh.'

Suddenly two shapes, one large, one small, rushed from behind the tree towards the lake. They moved with the speed of running dogs – for a moment Rachel thought they were dogs. But the large one was too large. And she saw as they crossed a patch of moonlight that their shape was wrong. They were low to the ground as hedgehogs – lower, as slugs. They slid down the lawn, down the bank, into the water without a splash, and were gone. A small ripple moved into the reeds and rocked the canoe.

She had felt Theo's arm reach round her and grab his camera. 'Too late. Damn.'

'What were they?'

'I don't know. But I'm not staying near the water.' He propelled the canoe forward. She clambered along the bow and jumped on the lawn. He followed, splashing in the reeds. Ahead, Rachel ran towards the stone wall at the front of the house.

'Rachel.'

She stopped.

'We've got to look for Mr Jones.'

'He hasn't called again.'

'He might be knocked out. Just a quick look. If he's in there we've got to try and save him.'

She had never been so frightened. But she followed him up the steps into the porch. 'I forgot my paddle.'

'Me too. Give me the torch.' He stood in the doorway and pointed it into the room. A blue light shone out from a small leaded window straight across from him. This was the light they had seen from the lake and from Rachel's bedroom. Round to one side ancient curtains, black and still as water in a well, hung from brass rings on a wooden bar fixed to a lintel. Their heavy dusty tassels drooped on the floor.

Three doors led out. Each was bolted and padlocked. The only other window was boarded over.

That was all – unless . . . Something in the back corner of the room caught his eye. He shone the torch at it. A trap-door lay open against the wall, with a dark hole leading down.

'If they've got him, he's either down there or behind that curtain.'

'I don't want to go in.'

'We've got to. Come on. The trapdoor first.'

They stepped into the room. At once they were struck by its coldness. Their skin seemed to shrink and the warmth drain out of their bodies before they had gone two steps. Then they felt a stickiness on their feet and lifting them saw their soles were coated with the same grey dust Uncle Clarry had found on his lawn.

'It's all over the floor.'

They crept to the trapdoor. Concrete steps went into the gloom, which seemed to swallow the light of the torch when Theo shone it down.

'I'm going to have a look.'

'No, Theo.'

'He might be down there. You stand at the top and shine the torch in.'

She knew that once he had started on something he would carry it through.

'I'll give you till I count twenty. Then I'm going.' She knelt on the floor and shone the torch into the cellar. Theo went down the steps.

'They're covered with dust. Phew, the stink. Like a dunny . . . Shine into the corners, Rachel.'

In a moment he gave a soft cry. 'There's a tunnel. I think it slopes down. Give me the torch.'

'Theo, they might come.'

'I've got to see in. Hurry up.'

She ran down the steps, her feet puffing up dust, and crossed to where Theo was kneeling in a corner. The mouth of the tunnel was round like a culvert and about a metre across. Rachel shone the torch into it.

'It goes down all right. Just a small slope,' Theo said. 'And it curves out of sight about five metres along.' He reached in and felt the walls. 'It's glass. Some sort of grey glass. I wish we could go down.'

'No, Theo.'

He put his head into the tunnel. 'Mr Jones,' he called softly, 'are you there?' His voice seemed to hiss and whisper and slide down into the dark. 'Mr Jones.'

'He's not there, Theo. Let's go.'

'All right.' He was reluctant. 'We'll have a look behind those curtains.'

Rachel started up the stairs. She shone the torch behind her to light him up. But he turned. He went back to the mouth of the tunnel and crouched, listening.

'There's a noise down there,' he whispered.

'Oh, do come on.'

'It's like a flight of ducks, high up.' Suddenly he felt a puff of cold air from the tunnel. It made his hair whisper about his ears. At the same time he heard a rushing slithering sound.

'Something's coming up. Quick, out.'

She kept the light on the steps until he was up. Then they ran to the door. The rushing sound was closer and the air forced from the tunnel raised dust in the cellar and lifted it like smoke through the trapdoor hole. 'Put the torch on it. I'm going to get a photo.' But Rachel had gone ahead into the porch. She ran back to his side. 'She's there, on the lawn. Mrs Wilberforce.'

A loud sudden quack came from the lake. They peered through the door. Beyond the shape of the woman on the lawn, silver water stretched to the opposite shore. They saw a dark shape on it, close to the foot of the hedge.

'It's the canoe. It must have floated out.'

Suddenly there was a cracking sound, a thrashing on the surface. The canoe vanished.

'It must be Mr Wilberforce. He's pulled it under.'

'Theo, *she's* coming inside.'

'Quick, behind the curtain.'

As they reached it something came with a wet explosion out of the tunnel in the cellar. The twins dived through the curtains and Theo held them with his hands to make them still. He peered through the gap into the room. Rachel stood behind him on tip-toe, stretching her neck to see over his head. Whatever it was that had come into the cellar was mounting the steps. It came up swiftly, with a sucking sound. In the blue light it bent into the room; eased over the top step; undulated towards the door. It was grey, glistening with oil and slime. Its shape was almost exactly slug-like; a little rounder, Theo thought, like a German helmet. It had a white bone beak, a black mouth, perfectly round, that ran like a drain into its body, and two blunt knobs in place of eyes. They glowed with a black radiance. As he watched another followed, then another. They slithered to the door and into the porch.

'What are they?'

'Slugs. Some sort of giant slugs.'

'Oh, Theo, how do we get out?'

'I don't know. One of them's by the steps, I think.'

They turned to face the room behind them. It was empty too. Blue light shone from under a door – the same light that glowed through the window in the other room. It showed a number of flattened piles of dust against the walls.

'Maybe they sleep on those.'

'Let's go. Please.'

'They've nailed boards over the windows.' He spoke calmly, but he was as terrified as her. He felt like curling up in a corner, hiding his head in his arms. But he pushed Rachel's shoulder, moved her towards the door. 'We'll go through there.' They had both forgotten Mr Jones.

They reached the door and listened for a moment. There was no sound on the other side. Theo took the handle. It turned easily. He opened the door with a push. At once they were flooded in light. It rushed out like water and washed all over them. They shielded their eyes and peered into it. Thousands of tiny stars floated in the room, tinier than gnats, than motes of dust, each one sending out its ounce of light. In places they were so thick they seemed to run together like swirls of mist. Apart from them the room was empty. It was a long narrow room, bare as a cell, and painted black – floor, walls, ceiling. A blind pulled over a window beyond the swarming stars was black as tar.

'Come on,' Theo whispered. He began to edge along the side of the room.

'What is it, Theo?'

'A galaxy, I think.' He got halfway along and saw one spiral arm was black. The dust motes in it sent out a radiation that touched his eyes like ice. Beyond it, separated by a metre of space, a second model came into view: a dozen balls, the size of marbles, circled about a sun. A solar system, he thought. One of the planets was black. He looked at it a moment, then went on to the window.

'How do they stay up?'

'I don't know. Don't touch them. They might be electric.'

Carefully he raised the blind until half the window was exposed. The panes were coated thickly with black paint. He saw a piece of dowelling set in a hole running through the window-sash into the frame. It acted as a bar so the window could not be raised. 'It's loose. You try and get it out. I'll do the catch.' But the catch had not been turned for many years. It was rusty and made grating sounds. At every one he stopped and listened. Outside on the lawn were quacking sounds.

'It's moving. Just a bit. If only I had some oil.'

'I've got this thing out.'

'Good. Hold me a minute. I'm going to spit on it.'

She supported him while he stood on the sill and spat several times on the catch. Then he worked at it again and suddenly it grated round and the window was free.

'Now slowly, so it doesn't squeak.'

Gently they worked the window up, one centimetre, two. Theo bent down and looked out. The light from the tiny stars spread across the lawn. 'Right, a bit more.'

But suddenly something huge and black rushed out from the shadow of a tree. It thumped like a sack of grain on the side of the house. A single angry quack sounded in the night.

Theo slammed the window shut. He grabbed the piece of dowelling from Rachel and rammed it in its hole. 'The slugs. They're out there.'

'Theo . . .'

'Yes.'

Their minds were working together now, rushing along the same line of thought. They had no time to wonder at it.

'Outside and down the steps. We'll split up. The one who gets away calls the police.'

'I'm scared, Theo.'

'Me too. I'm sorry I got you into this. You go straight up the path and over the wall. I'll duck around and try to make them follow me.'

They edged quickly by the models, ran through the room with the piles of dust, thrust open the curtains. And there, in the porch entrance, dripping with water, was Mr Wilberforce. His deep eyes glowed with a strange cold light and his wooden mouth smiled. 'Welcome, children. No, don't run. There's nowhere you can run to.'

'Where's Mr Jones?' Theo whispered.

'Did you think that was him? Oh no. That was me calling you.'

'Who are you?'

'That doesn't matter. This is the end for you.'

His face began to change and his body sink towards the floor. His nose slowly changed into a beak.

'Theo, he's turning himself into a slug.'

'The cellar,' Theo cried. 'Run.'

Their sudden dash away from him took Mr Wilberforce by surprise. He was still more man than slug; and he tried to go back to his human shape. It slowed his movements. Rachel ran part-way down the steps. She waited as Theo reached up and caught the edge of the trapdoor. Mr Wilberforce saw what they meant to do. He lurched heavily forward.

'Shine the torch in his eyes,' Theo cried.

The beam struck the man squarely in the face, showing muddy eyes set deep in caves. He gave a grunt that might have been of pain and flung up his hands. Theo worked the trapdoor to its point of balance. The man, the slug, came forward.

'Duck,' Theo yelled. He pulled the trapdoor down. It fell like lead and thumped him on the back, knocking him off the stairs into the dust below. It was Rachel who rammed home the heavy bolt, just as the door gave a groan and jerked upwards in the middle. It jerked again, again. The man above was pulling in a frenzy. Then a huge weight settled on the door. Its timber creaked and bent.

'Is it going to hold?' Theo's voice came weakly from the floor.

'I think so. Till they get something to break it.' She came down the steps and crouched beside him. 'Are you all right?'

'A bit winded. It missed my head.'

'Where do we go from here? Don't answer. I know. Theo, something's happened to us. We don't seem to need words. I can hear what you're thinking.'

'I can hear you too. We've got to go down there, Rachel. Down the tunnel.'

'What if there's water? We'll drown.'

'That's better than waiting here for them.'

'Can we throw something down first and hear if there's a splash?'

He got up painfully and limped to the tunnel. 'There might be more of them down there. I'm sorry. Don't cry.'

'I can't help it. I just . . . don't want to be . . . caught.'

'We'll get out. Can you find my camera? Bring it over here.'

She wiped her cheeks and watched him in the torch-light. He knelt beside the tunnel and placed the camera on its lip.

'You'll lose your pictures.'

'They're not important now. Anyway, we're going to the same place.'

'Listen to them quack. They're planning something.' There was a great slithering sound above. The weight went off the door. Then there was silence. 'Oh, please be quick.'

He shoved the camera forward as hard as he could. It slid easily on the glass, almost soundlessly. He pulled her hand with the torch down and they watched the small black case speed to the corner and turn quickly out of sight. They waited. The tunnel kept the faint sound alive for a moment, but soon it died. Then there was nothing. The camera had simply gone – down – into darkness – into nothingness it seemed.

'Is it our turn now?'

'Yes.'

The silence above was more frightening than the darkness below.

Theo sat on the lip of the tunnel. The glass felt like ice on his legs and was so slippery that for a moment he thought he was sliding away. Rachel took hold of his collar. She sat behind him.

'Give me the torch,' Theo said. 'Now put your legs around me. And your arms. Wherever we're going we'd better arrive together. Are you all set?'

'Yes.'

'Shove yourself forward then.'

5. 'A TUNNEL'S GOT TO GO SOMEWHERE'

She pushed herself on to the glass and at once they shot forward at a speed that made them cry out with surprise. They went round the first bend and the slope grew steeper. Theo had trouble keeping the torch steady. Their momentum forced them down on their backs. Rachel could see nothing. She held Theo's collar. Several times his weight almost dragged him away from her. He had to let go the torch to keep his grip on her legs. It fell behind them, turning slowly, lighting the tunnel then leaving it in darkness.

They went down like a sled in an ice-chute, swinging up the sides on every turn. The bends drew tighter, corkscrewing, then seemed to widen out. It was impossible to count them, but to Theo it seemed they must have dropped almost a hundred metres. The slope grew gentler then and the tunnel straightened out. He guessed they were being carried under the lake. The torch followed round the bend and lighted the tunnel sides for a moment but their own huge shadow blotted out whatever lay ahead.

They burst into the open like a train from a tunnel. Clouds of choking dust rose about them. The torch came down and thumped the back of Rachel's head. She cried out. Then a silence fell so intense they could almost hear the beating of their hearts. In a moment they were able to open their eyes. They scrambled up and held on to each other. The dust began to settle.

They were in a huge room, a chamber as large as a school assembly hall. It seemed to be hollowed out of stone. A grey light filled it, so dull they had trouble seeing each other, yet painful, intense. They were forced to peer about through half-closed lids. Floating midway between ceiling and floor, taking up more than half the space in the room, was a huge grey-brown balloon – no, not a balloon, a globe, a planet, turning lazily at a pace the twins could have kept up with by walking. The grey light shone from it and was reflected back from the stone walls. The globe had no life. Yet it moved, it hung without support, held by a force that must, Theo thought, be generated in its interior. He went towards it slowly. Its surface made him shudder – so gluey-looking, so cold.

'Don't touch it.'

'Why not?'

Their voices echoed in the chamber, seemed to round the globe and pounce on them from the other side. They spoke after that without making sounds, without realizing fully what they were doing.

'It might be dangerous. Electric.'

'I don't think so. It's just – I feel as if I'll pick up germs if I touch it.'

He reached out his hand all the same. His fingers sank into the globe's surface and came away coated with slime. 'It's freezing. Like cold porridge. Why doesn't it fall off if it's so thin?'

'What is it?'

'Mud, I think.'

'There's something sticking up. It looks like mountains.'

A ridge of stone stood up from the mud. It moved slowly past their eyes, a dozen metres out of Theo's reach.

'There's another.' Soon they made out many more, grey on the paler grey of the mud. There were single peaks, and ridges that twisted across the surface like snakes.

'There's a smooth one.'

'That's not a mountain.'

It was a bubble of grey glass about the size of a pudding bowl, rising from the mud and gleaming dully. 'There's one down here.' They counted seven.

'What are they?'

'I don't know . . . I think this is maybe – the world they come from.'

'The slugs? They live in mud?'

He shrugged. 'I might as well get a photo.'

They hunted in the dust by the tunnel entrance and found his camera not far from the torch. Rachel shone the beam on a mountain range, then on one of the glass bubbles, while Theo took photographs.

'They probably won't come out. There's dust all over the lens.'

'Theo, I'm not so scared now. I'm remembering bits of the afternoon. Are you?'

'I can remember most of it. It looks as if we've broken through his barrier. But that doesn't help us out of here.'

'What do you call a thing with seven sides?'

'I'm not sure. Heptagon, I think. Or heptahedron. Why?'

'I can see my stone. In a blurry sort of way. It comes and goes.'

'I can see something too. Shining.'

'It's got seven sides. It's red – like a huge ruby.'

'Mine's blue. I can see it in time with my heartbeat.'

'Do you think he'll be angry? Us remembering? And learning to pebble again?'

'I don't think he'll ever know. We're trapped in here.'

'There might be other tunnels.'

They walked around the globe, keeping their eyes on the wall. There were two more openings. Both had the appearance of culverts and both had the same grey lining.

'This one goes down, the same as the one in the cellar. It

must go deeper under the lake. I wonder what's down there.'

'I don't want to find out. Theo, can you hear anything?'

He listened. 'No.'

'I thought I heard that quacking sound again. Far away.'

'Come on. Let's try the other.'

The second tunnel ran straight and flat. They walked along it bent from the waist, with their hair brushing the ceiling.

'Which way is it going?'

'I don't know. I'm hoping it'll come out on the other side of the lake. Maybe they own another house.'

'How long will it take them to break the trapdoor?'

'Not long. But I think there's probably another entrance. Maybe down in the lake. That's the only reason for them swimming.'

'This could be the entrance.'

'I know. We could meet them coming.'

'How far have we gone?'

'Not far. A hundred metres.'

Their thoughts went back and forth more quickly than spoken words. They took comfort from it. It was hard to believe they could be captured now. It would be such a waste. Yet they could not see how they were to escape. The only thing to do was to keep going.

The tunnel began to turn left and gradually climb. Their feet began to slip.

'Get down and crawl.'

'The torch gets in the way.'

'Put it in your shirt.'

But the slope grew steeper. Even crawling they made little progress. They had to press their palms so hard on the tunnel floor that soon their arms were aching too much for them to go on.

'Try turning side on. Put your feet on one wall and your back on the other. Is that easier?'

'A bit.'

But as she spoke her lower hand skidded from under her. She slid back, collided with Theo, and together they careered back down the slope and ten metres along the flat.

'All right. Try again. Take it slower this time.'

They made painful progress. Twice Rachel slipped but Theo had braced himself firmly enough to hold them.

'How far have we come now?'

'I haven't got a clue. But we must be close to the other side of the lake. If that's the way we're going.'

'Quiet, Theo.'

'I'm not talking. Remember?'

'Quiet.'

They both listened intently. The sounds she had heard came again – a distant quacking.

'Be still. Don't make a sound.'

The quacking grew louder, and suddenly its volume doubled.

'They've come into the big room.'

For a moment there was no sound. Then a single quack. Then nothing again.

'Where do you think they are?'

'I'm not sure. They must have come up from below. So maybe they've gone back down. Or they might be in the other tunnel – the one going up to the cellar. That means they'll open the trapdoor.'

'Oh, Theo –'

'Get going. And for God's sake don't slip.'

They started their sideways progress again. Behind them the silence was complete.

'Theo, it's flattening out.'

'Keep going.'

'It's level. Wait, I'm going to use the torch.'

She took it out of her shirt and shone it ahead.

'Theo,' she wailed.

'What is it?' He peered past her, and saw. The tunnel simply ended. A short way ahead the grey glass curved down, up, in from either side, and closed like the bottom of a test tube.

'We're trapped.'

'But that's impossible. There's no sense in it. A tunnel's got to go somewhere.'

They crawled to the end, shone the torch about, felt the walls, and then crouched, defeated. There was no argument. They were caught like flies in a bottle.

'I'm not going back. I'm not going down that other one.'

'Nor me . . . It's too late anyway.'

They had both heard it: a quacking, a slithering sound. The air about them seemed to turn to ice.

'Keep the torch going.'

The quacking stopped, but the sliding sound grew louder, grew into a gluey, squeaky hiss. The twins pressed themselves into the end of the tunnel. Rachel kept the torch pointed at the place where the slugs would appear. Theo held his camera by its strap to use as a weapon.

Two of the creatures appeared, side by side. They were small. The ones that had come out of the cellar had been the size of forty-gallon drums. These were scarcely a metre long. But there was no mistaking their menace. They had stopped at the top of the slope. Now they began to slide forward. The two knobs on their front – eyes or nose, the twins could not tell – pulsed from black to red. They came slowly, inching forward, stopped a moment to quack – a question? an answer? – slid forward again; but slower now.

'It's the light. I think it hurts them.'

'It's not going to stop them though.'

He reached forward and swung his camera. It was an awkward blow but it made the slugs ooze back. The camera struck the tunnel floor with a smashing sound.

'There go my pictures.'

'They're scared, Theo. These ones must be babies.'

'They're coming back. They're splitting up.'

The slugs were sliding different ways, one up either wall of the tunnel.

'I can't cover them both.'

'Just keep the torch straight ahead.'

He struck again. This time the camera caught one of the slugs in the middle of its back but it simply bounced off like a rubber ball. The slug quacked. Its companion answered. They had learned something. Again they moved forward.

'Theo,' Rachel cried, 'think light. Quickly. A searchlight. Flood the tunnel with light.'

'How . . .'

'With your mind, you dummy. Light. Light. Concentrate.'

They threw their minds into it. They made a beam — white, searing, strong enough to light a city street, and although they could see no change with their eyes, although the feeble torch-light still made its yellow pool in the tunnel, in their minds everything was scorched, was held in a pitiless glare. They poured the full force of it straight at the slugs.

For a moment nothing happened. Then the two creatures curled up at the edges, tried to fold their bodies to shield their 'eyes'. They backed off, turned, slid away blindly, quacking with terror or pain. The twins followed them to the top of the slope and kept the beam pointing down the tunnel. Only when the slugs were out of sight, when there was no more sound, did they relax. At once they felt exhausted. They almost fell, and Theo had to grab Rachel's arm to stop her from sliding away down the tunnel. The torch fell from her hand and sped away, but it did not seem important now. They crawled back to the end of the tunnel and lay close together, curled up.

'My head's aching,' Theo whispered.

'Mine too. Do you think they've gone to let the others in?'

'I think the bolt's too high. They're baby ones.'

They lay quiet for another moment. Rachel said, 'I can't see my stone any more.'

'We've used up our strength. It wouldn't work against Mr Wilberforce anyhow. It might hurt him but it wouldn't stop him.'

'What are we going to do?'

'I'm too tired to think. I want to go to sleep.'

'Don't, Theo. We've got to get out. You said there must be a reason for this tunnel. A hidden entrance.'

'I felt everywhere.'

'Why isn't it dark?'

'It is dark.'

'Open your eyes. There's a sort of light in the ceiling.' He opened them, then sat up slowly. He felt his tiredness melt away. The roof of the tunnel was rippling, flickering. A faint yellow light came through it from something that glowed fuzzily, like a veiled electric bulb.

'It's the moon, Theo. I know it is.'

'It could be just another one of their models.'

'It's the moon shining through water. We're under the lake.'

'But we've come too far down. We can't be that close to the surface.' He put his hand up cautiously and touched the ceiling, then drew it back. His fingers were sticky with some sort of semi-transparent jelly.

'That wouldn't keep water out.'

Again he put up his hand and this time pushed it in. It went deeper, up to his wrist, his elbow, almost to his shoulder. He gave a small cry and drew it back. 'I came out the other side. It's water, I think.' He tried again.

'It's water all right. This stuff's only about half a metre through. Wait a minute.' He bent his wrist down and felt all around with his fingers. 'It's hard on top. Like rock. It must be like that one-way glass. You can put your arm through it this way but not the other, so the water doesn't get in. They must have some way of reversing it when they come in from outside.'

'Can we get through?'

'I don't see why not. We've got to try, anyway.'

'How deep do you think the water is?'

'Don't worry about that. Just hold your breath and swim like mad for the surface.'

'Can I go first? I couldn't stand being here by myself.'

'I'm not sure I can either.'

'Please, Theo.'

'O.K. Put your foot in my hands. I'm going to heave you right through. It's soft, so don't be scared.'

For a moment they stood poised like a pair of gymnasts. Then Theo heaved Rachel up. Her head and shoulders disappeared through the ceiling. He took the soles of her feet in a harder grip and gave a second heave. The light of the moon was partly blotted out. He saw her shadow moving in the water, then flattening out as it reached the surface. There was no sound in the tunnel. He crouched and listened. Then he reached up and plunged his arm into the jelly. He took a hold of its hard upper surface, and saw at once that he had not understood the difficulty of getting out of the tunnel without help. He would have to push both arms through, get an elbow out on the surface and lever himself up. That meant his face would be in the jelly for as long as the operation took. He went cold at the thought. But it had to be done. He stuffed the broken camera down his shirt, pushed both arms into the jelly, took a hold, and started to pull himself up. It took all the strength he had. The jelly pressed against his mouth, into his nose. He struggled to get an elbow on to the ledge, but the jelly was heavy, it slowed him. He fell back, gulped in air, scraped the slime from his face. Above,

73

Rachel circled, waiting. He tried again. This time he managed. He got an elbow out and levered on his forearm. His face broke through into water. But still he could not breathe and now he was desperate. It seemed to have taken minutes to get this far. He got his palms flat down, thrust as hard as he could, felt for the jelly surface with his foot, and thrust again. His buoyancy helped now. His other foot came free. Paddling and kicking madly, he made for the surface. He broke through into dazzling light, into air that was sharp with salt.

Rachel caught his shoulder. 'I thought you weren't coming. We're in the sea.'

The air seemed almost liquid. He took it into his throat in long gulps. 'I nearly – got stuck. I thought I was – a goner.'

'It's Thornes Bay. There are the rocks. Come on, Theo. Before they come after us.'

She let go his shoulder and started to dog-paddle towards the shore. He followed, using the same stroke. The water was silver with moonlight. Rocks were piled on either side of a short grey beach. They made for the nearer ones, less than a hundred metres away. The tide was at its lowest. Soon they were able to wade. They pulled themselves on to the rocks and crouched there shivering. The sky behind Rangitoto was gathering a faint colour between yellow and grey. It was almost dawn.

'Let's get home.'

Before they could move they heard the sound of a car coming down the road towards the beach. Lights glowed at the top of the bank.

'Down. As low as you can get.' Rachel was in charge now. Theo was dazed, still in a state of shock from his struggle to get through the jelly. He knelt on the jagged stone, feeling nothing, with his head buried in his arms.

Rachel watched between two walls of rock. The car lights

went out, the engine noise stopped. A door opened and closed. The figure that hurried down the steps to the beach was one she could not mistake.

'It's Mr Wilberforce.'

Theo stirred slightly.

The man ran over the sand to the water and ploughed some distance into it. He knelt down. He was still and black as a rock. She guessed he was changing shape, getting ready to swim. In a moment he moved forward. She could not see what shape he had taken, he was like a black log on the water, making a silver wave. Then he plunged and was gone.

'He's heading towards the tunnel. Come on, Theo.'

He got to his feet. She helped him out of the rocks.

'Now run. Straight for home. As fast as you can go.'

They ran. They ran. Across the sand, up the steps, past the black car, along footpaths, past hedges, gates, dark houses, through puddles of light under lamp-posts, thinking of one thing only – home.

They burst into the living-room. Rachel slammed the door behind her and fastened the safety chain.

The lights were on. Uncle Clarry poked his head out of the kitchen.

'Where in God's name did you two come from? I thought you were in bed.'

'We went for a swim.'

'At this hour? You pair of flipping idiots. In your clothes too.' He looked at them closely. 'What's the matter with him?'

'It was colder than we thought.'

'Well, get into the shower. Both of you. I'll make you a drink.'

Rachel brought down their pyjamas. The shower warmed them. Theo got back some colour. But he was groggy with tiredness.

Uncle Clarry took them into the kitchen and gave them a hot chocolate drink.

'A friend of mine's calling for me. We're heading off for a day's fishing. So you kids behave yourself. Don't you go worrying Noeline with stunts like this.'

'No, Uncle.'

'O.K. Off to the sack then.'

They went. They pulled their blankets up over their heads and slept as though they had been stunned with rubber truncheons.

6. HOW THE WAR BEGAN ...

Aunt Noeline called them at nine o'clock. She told them she was disappointed in them for sneaking out. Didn't they know it was dangerous swimming at night? And what would their parents have thought if they'd caught pneumonia?

They pebbled back and forth to keep up their spirits. When breakfast was over they set off for Mr Jones's. They kept off side streets and went around through the town.

'I've been thinking,' Theo said as they walked along, 'those models – the big one in the house was a galaxy. The Wilberforces must own the part they've coloured black.'

Rachel shivered. 'What about the other one?'

He looked at her. 'A solar system. Not just any one. Saturn was there. Remember the ring? And the asteroid belt. The black one was number three.'

'What does that mean?'

'It was the Earth. And the Wilberforces think it belongs to them.'

'So the model in the big hall . . .'

'Yes. Those mountains were the Himalayas. And the Andes. The Southern Alps were there.'

'What were the glass things?'

'Cities, maybe.'

'Can they do it, Theo? All that mud? What are they?'

'That's what Mr Jones is going to tell us.' He felt very grim.

They came to the white cottage. The gate jingled as they opened it. At once the old man's face was at the window. They felt something jab into their minds. His face disappeared and a moment later the door flew open.

'Come in. Quickly.' He shunted them into the kitchen. 'Sit down. Now tell me.'

It tumbled out: the slugs, the smell, the quacking, the voice that called for help – and the models, the cellar, the tunnels under the lake. Sometimes they pebbled together, but Mr Jones could hear it all. Once he groaned, and once his eyes filled with tears and he rubbed them away angrily with his hand. Rachel knew he was thinking of the twins who had died. But when they told him how they had driven the baby slugs away by making a beam of light with their minds his face began to get its colour back.

'You can see the stones?'

'A little bit.'

'A bit.'

'Why did we remember like that, after you made us forget?'

'You're stronger than I thought. But it was fear gave you the push you needed. They've helped us, our friends the Wilberforces. But they know now. They know what you are. I mustn't be careless again.'

'Would they have killed us?'

'The way you'd crush a snail. I'm sorry, Rachel, I'm not trying to frighten you. But you must know these things.'

'Will they come after us again?'

'They'll be waiting their chance. But don't worry. I'll be guarding you. I'll be watching every minute. If we're careful there's nothing they can do.'

'Why do they want to kill us? Is it to stop us telling people?'

'The stones,' Theo said.

'Yes. The stones. Because you can use them. You told me yesterday, Rachel, they were a weapon. But they're not a weapon just for anyone. Only you. Only Theo.'

'Against the Wilberforces?'

'Against the Wilberforces.'

'Why, though? Are they hurting anyone?' But as she said this she remembered the model of the Earth reduced to mud, and knew the answer. Mr Jones nodded. 'That's what they plan to do, Rachel, not only here but right through the universe. And the only people who can stop them are you and Theo. I know, it makes you feel helpless. Two children on an unimportant planet. But that's how it's fallen out. If you succeed, your race has a future. If not – the Wilberforces.'

'Isn't there anyone who can help?'

'No one, my dear. No one.'

She felt tiny, like an insect, like a creature on which some huge crushing weight might descend at any moment. Her skin seemed to shrink and turn cold. Mr Jones reached out and touched her hand. But the warmth travelled only to her wrist. It had no strength against the dread that filled her.

Theo, meanwhile, had been on a different course. The two white stones rested on the window sill. The left hand one flickered like a blinky neon tube. That was his. It took momentarily a pale blue colour and a seven-sided shape. He wanted an explanation. And an explanation for the Wilberforces. It was more than time.

He said, 'What are the Wilberforces? Can you tell us? And what are you?'

Mr Jones smiled. 'Theo the practical one. You were very brave last night, Theo. Even if you weren't very sensible. You too, Rachel. But you want an answer. What are the Wilberforces?' He sighed. 'What are they? I can't tell it – not

79

in words. I'll have to show you. Open your minds. And don't be frightened. I'm here.'

They saw a huge blue sun and, turning majestically about it, a single planet. They swooped down on it like birds and hovered over the surface. It was a world partly of mud, partly stone – a black and iron-grey world: seas of mud, continents of stone. Huge worm-like creatures wallowed in the shallows and along the estuaries. They were the size of battleships, yet the twins guessed their brains were peanut-sized. They were blind, mouthless, iron-skinned, indestructible.

'They have no name,' Mr Jones said. 'They don't need a name. Harmless creatures – they simply existed.'

'What do they live on?'

'The mud. It's full of minerals that filter through the skin along their bellies. So really, you see, they're swimming in their food. They had no future. They would have died out like your dinosaurs if it hadn't been for these creatures on the land.'

They swung inland, over the continents of stone, and here, in caves, in tunnels, in the dark, were the slug-creatures the twins had seen at the Wilberforces'. They were nomadic, they lived in bands, they used their bodies as men use weapons and tools.

'But they had no future either,' Mr Jones said. 'Their world was too barren. They were in a blind alley. Until they discovered these creatures in the sea. It was many millions of years ago, Rachel. But when they found them it was like finding a new world. The . . .'

'Yes?'

'Have you heard of symbiosis?'

'A sort of joining together?'

'Two organisms joining, each one depending on the other. The Wilberforces joined with these big worms in the mud. It took many thousands of years. But what they decide on they do. They became the brain in a huge body more powerful than any machine ever made, in a sea of food that seemed to have no end. And then after thousands more years they began to spread out through the stars. They're creatures of tremendous will – no imagination, no feeling, no conscience. They remind me of some of the leaders of your race. But ambition, will – there have never been creatures like them. And all turned to a single cause – to destroy, to multiply. Their name, well, call them the Wilberforces – although Wilberforce is too good for them. You could never pronounce the name they gave themselves, but it means *People of the mud, who conquer and multiply.* See how they spread.'

The twins saw grey-domed cities rise on that planet of mud. They saw mighty star-ships leap out. They saw new stars, with green planets turning about them. The ships landed, the blind worms wriggled out, each ridden by its brain. Devastation, death. And from the huge factories that sprang up there trundled fantastic machines that chewed each planet to mud. On and on it went, across a whole arm of the galaxy. The planets turned from green to brown to grey.

'There was nothing left when they finished with a world. Not an insect. Not a blade of grass. Just mud and stone. And the Wilberforces. Nothing could stop them. Until they landed on one of the planets where my people lived.'

The twins sighed. They had been waiting for this. It was all that had stopped them from curling up. Mr Jones sighed too.

'I can't show you much. We're a people dead and gone and memory is painful. But look.'

They saw a world like their own – green continents, blue seas. And small cities, each like a filigree of silver, shining in valleys and along the sides of lakes. The old man took them no closer. Yet they had a sense of life flickering in those

81

cities, moving like blue and yellow flames, swiftly and lightly.

'That is where we began. We spread out too, to other planets, but more in curiosity than conquest. We didn't go very far, there seemed no need.' He sighed again. 'We believed we had the secret of eternal life – and so we had no young. There seemed no need for that either.' He laughed. 'We were a dying race, although we didn't know it. Well, the Wilberforces gave us a little extra time. We came alive for a spell – long enough to stop them in their tracks and turn them back.'

'What are you called?' Theo asked.

'Oh, it doesn't matter now. A name. It meant *The People who understand*. We suffered from pride, you see. Jones will do very well now.'

'How did you fight them?'

'With magic. With spells. That was our science. We had learned to harness the powers of the mind. But magic is what we must call it. And we simply tied the Wilberforces up, we dropped a net of magic over them. They were paralysed until the end of time – or so we thought. We traced them back planet by planet, caught them in our net, left them – and the planets turned green again. New life appeared, and the Wilberforces lay about like so many petrified logs.'

He let them see that: the greening planets, the huge worms lying where the spell had caught them – soon under the shade of trees, tangled in creepers, scurried over by small new furry creatures.

'And then we began to die ourselves. Our immortality was a dream. Our fight with the Wilberforces had kept us alive, oh, for many more thousands of years than we deserved, but it had taken the last of our strength as well. Almost the last. We came back to our home planet, the few of us who were left. And there we learned of the cunning of

82

the Wilberforces. We had taken them too lightly. We had not studied them well. But they had studied us – and at the end a few, very few, had begun to master our science. They had learned magic. A rough, crude magic. But enough to manufacture a counter-spell.'

He walked about the room. He suddenly seemed very frail – a small withered old man with nothing special about him.

'It wasn't your fault,' Rachel said.

'We had been so pleased with ourselves, for so long. And so arrogant. *The People who understand*. Well, the Wilberforces taught us a lesson.'

'What did they do?'

'There were only seven of them, the ones who had learned. But of course we knew nothing of that. We had tracked them down, along with all the others. A family – the father, the mother, three sons, two daughters. On the farthest planet of all. The smell – you've smelt it, Rachel, Theo. It's in your minds, not real for other people. But it spreads across the stars and by following it we can find the Wilberforces. And we had found them here, on this isthmus. Burrowed in. The father here, see, and the mother here . . .'

They were hovering over a wooded neck of land between two harbours. It took them a moment to recognize it – no city, no wharves, no bridge. Rangitoto had a different shape and trees grew on the slopes of Mount Eden and One Tree Hill. The Maoris had not arrived. A dreadful stillness shimmered in the air – and the smell of the Wilberforces floated up.

Again they did not see the Joneses, but they saw lines of light so dense it seemed to be liquid. A net of light floated in the sky, knotted in seven places. As they watched it settled down, gentle as rain, and melted into the earth and into the sea. Where the knots descended they knew the Wilberforces were hidden: under North Head and Mount Victoria, under One Tree Hill, Mount Wellington, Mount Eden, under Rangitoto, under Lake Pupuke.

'We bound them. And then we left,' Mr Jones said. 'We thought our job was done. But even before we were out of your atmosphere their counter-spell was working.'

'What was it?' Theo whispered.

'Rough magic – primitive. Compared with ours it was like a stone axe alongside a laser beam. But it worked. Like everything the Wilberforces did.'

'How?'

'It freed them cell by cell, like unravelling knitting. Time means nothing to them. It has taken thousands of years. They wait – they simply wait. And cell by cell they break out of our spell. The brain comes first – the part you call the slugs. And they are able to free themselves from the bodies, the giant worms. When those are free they'll join again, and breed, and turn your world into mud. And set out again to destroy the universe.'

'How long have we got?'

'They're close, Theo. Very close. The Wilberforces are getting careless. They know they can't be stopped. It might be as close as months, or even weeks.'

After the thousands of years, the isthmus without people, the Rangitoto that had not finished erupting, it did not seem possible to be so near the end.

'But somebody must have seen them before – in all those years. The Maoris. The settlers. There's half a million people here.'

'They've only come out in the last few years, Theo. Two of them have learned to take human shape – the father and the mother. It takes tremendous effort but they can do it. They can take any shape you like to name – a tree, an animal, a man. The policeman you see in the street could be Mr Wilberforce. They want to find out about the surface, you see. So that when they come up they'll know what they have to face. What is it, Rachel?'

'Can't we talk to them? Can't we persuade them to go away? To another planet? If there are so many planets?'

'They don't want one, they want the lot. They want to breed. Remember their name – *The People who conquer and multiply*. There's no room for anyone else.'

'But if we could talk to them –'

'You might just as well try talking to a school of sharks.'

The example made her shiver. It disturbed the old man too for he turned away sharply and said, 'There are things I don't want to remember. Let me finish my story.' He came to his chair and sat down.

'We learned what they were doing. We could still smell them, you see, across all those light years of space. And we made our last effort. Our dying effort. We poured all of our knowledge, all of our skill, into a weapon that would destroy them. Not simply throw them into a sleep until the end of time. Destroy. We made the stones. Those two pebbles on the window-sill. We poured into those all the remaining energies of our race. And then the last two of us, the only ones not on the point of death, set out again to find the last of the Wilberforces. We came here. The war had come down to that. Seven Wilberforces, two Joneses.'

He shook his head and said nothing.

'What happened?' Theo said.

He shook his head again. 'Oh, nothing.'

'Nothing?'

'Nothing, Theo. It had been too long a journey. I was the younger, the stronger, but my companion was old. He fought to stay alive – but as I said, it was too long a journey.'

'He died?'

'Yes, Rachel. We landed. We set out to use our weapon. But before we could use it, he died.'

'So you're the last one left.'

'Yes. The last. The last of *The People who understand*.'

'But why didn't *you* use the stones?' Theo burst out. 'By yourself?'

'It wasn't so simple, Theo. Our magic depends upon poles. Opposites. Two stones — two people to use them. And not just any two. I could not use them with any member of my race — just my companion. And I couldn't use them with you. Or you, Rachel.'

Theo was silent. At last the old man said, 'But I stay alive. Utterly helpless. I can go anywhere. They can't keep me out of their tunnels and caves. I sit under their mountains and brood. I stand on the backs of their worms. But I can do nothing. I've learned to take this human shape. I've even come to like it. It's hard for me now to turn back into myself. I'm almost human. It's less lonely like that.'

'Oh, Mr Jones,' Rachel said.

But Theo interrupted. 'Not helpless,' he said. 'That's a lot of hooey, isn't it?'

'Hooey?'

'Rubbish, I mean. Bullswool. Be quiet, Rachel.'

'Why is it rubbish?'

'Because you found those other twins. And you found us. And *we* can use the stones. Isn't that right?'

7. THE SWEDISH TWINS

'So let's get started, ' he said.

The old man laughed. 'Theo brings us down to earth.' But his face had taken a more lively expression. 'He's right, Rachel. We aren't beaten. They're close to breaking free, those worms of ours, but we've got one last chance to lay them low.'

He went to the window, picked up the stones, and came back to his chair. 'I've been more than four hundred years on your world and in that time I've found only one other pair who could use them. I've hunted in every land. But only one pair. And now two. Twins. Red-heads – red is our colour. Opposites. And with the gift of "speaking". I thought because you weren't identical it mightn't work – but see . . .' He held the stones out on his palms.'. . . they want to go to you. They want to be used.'

The stones were flickering – at least, the one in his left hand was flickering for Rachel, from white to reddish-yellow, from oval to seven-sided, and the one in his right for Theo, in shape, in colour – white to blue. They felt warmth radiating from them, and they reached out their hands.

'No,' Mr Jones said. 'Things have changed since yesterday. You've come a long way – the mud-people have pushed you through whole generations of change. You're not the same Rachel and Theo Matheson. But there's still a long way to go. You can't touch these again until you can see them. Absolutely steady. And you've got to see every side at once. All seven sides. And see yourself looking in from every one. And you've got to see the colour – rich and dark, and yet as clear as water.'

He looked steadily at them. The stones flickered and threw out their warmth.

'And when you can do that you've got to hold them. And that will hurt. You've got to endure the hurt – and wait – until it grows less. It will go away in the end.'

Silence again. They could hear themselves breathing.

At last Theo said, 'All right. I think we understand. What happens then? When we can hold them how do we use them?'

'One thing at a time, Theo. I'll show you how to use them – but first, you show me you can hold them.'

'All right.'

He reached out his hand and picked up the blue pebble. But at once he yelled with pain and jerked his hand in the air. The stone fell on the floor and lay there flickering.

'It's red-hot.'

'You're too fast, Theo. Learn to see it first. Then it will not be so hot. Not quite so hot.' Mr Jones was smiling but he had gone pale. He reached down and picked up the stone.

'Now look at them. Concentrate. Forget your hand, Theo, the pain's gone now. Look at your stone. Seven sides. Take it in your mind. Let it know it belongs to you – you're the boss. Tell it to keep still. Tell it to stop flickering. You too, Rachel. See it clear, see it still, see it whole.'

Theo stared – he stared – he stared – until he could feel himself going cross-eyed. Rachel seemed further ahead. Her eyes were very wide, absolutely still. Her stone to him was a white egg lying on Mr Jones's palm, but he could tell that to her it was a heptahedron, yellow-red, blinking only slightly, clear as glass, rich as the skin of an orange, reflecting her face to her from each of its seven mirrors. He was not going to be left behind. He concentrated harder. He tried to bore into his stone and look out from the inside. He pretended he was a geologist with a tiny hammer, tapping the surface trying to find a way in – and slowly, as the rhythmical sound played on his mind, the image faded, the stone grew larger, it seemed to invade his head. Its flickering became less regular, its shape could be seen for longer and longer periods. Its colour was the colour of the sky, and yet of the sea, and of delphiniums – but it was one colour only, clear as water, thick and rich as paint. He sighed with the pleasure of looking at it. But soon, though he knew he should not, he questioned it. What are you? he murmured, how am I supposed to use you? And the stone flickered madly and lost its shape. He came out of his trance with an exclamation of disappointment.

'Well done, Theo,' Mr Jones said. 'You went a long way. You very nearly had it.'

Theo shook his head. Something seemed to be wrong. The sun was slanting differently through the window. He looked at his watch. An hour and a quarter had passed.

'Hey!'

'Don't be frightened.'

'I thought it was only a minute.' He saw that Mr Jones was sitting at the table now and the stones were on the arms of the chair he had left. 'How did you move without us seeing?'

'You were very deep down, Theo.'

'What about Rachel?'

'She's doing very well. Very well indeed.'

She was sitting exactly as he had seen her last – wide-eyed, still as a lizard on a rock. He felt if he looked hard enough he would see the line of her sight spearing out to her stone.

'I'm going to try again.'

'Good boy. Relax. Take it slowly. You shouldn't need your little hammer this time.'

And this was so. His mind was ready and he held the stone easily in its embrace – blue, seven-sided, steady – almost steady. It *would* flicker just when he believed he had it. But he saw it from every side at once. He saw it from inside and out. The moments when it lost shape, when it became again just a white river-bed pebble, were painful. He felt them like the sting of a rubber band. How long it went on he did not know. A soft voice began to sound in his mind. 'Theo, Theo.'

'What?'

'You can come out now.'

It was Mr Jones. Theo shivered. He was suddenly very tired and he realized that this was the hardest work he had ever done. He blinked and swayed a little. Rachel was grinning at him. She had a bottle of Fanta in her hand. More than anything he wanted a drink. Mr Jones reached out with another bottle.

'Here you are, Theo. It's dry work.'

He drank, letting the ice-cold liquid pour down his throat until the bottle was half empty.

'Now have some chocolate. You've used up a lot of energy.'

'What time is it?'

'It's nearly lunch-time, Theo,' Rachel said. 'But we don't have to go. I rang Auntie. And Mr Jones talked to her too, so that's all right. She even said we could stay for tea.' She laughed excitedly. 'I did better than you. I can hold mine fifteen seconds without a flicker. You can only do twelve.'

'Who told you that?'

'He did.'

'It's not a competition,' Mr Jones said. 'You're a team. The two stones work together. Now you finish your drinks while I get lunch. You can look at those' – he motioned at the stones on the arms of the chair – 'but don't try to pick them up.'

Theo put out a finger and stopped it an inch or two away from his stone. Heat came off as though from the element of a stove. He felt depressed. It seemed no cooler than before.

Mr Jones gave them boiled eggs and thick tomato sandwiches. He ate nothing himself but paced about the room. He seemed unable to keep still and once or twice the twins caught him looking at them with something like pity.

'Don't you eat the same food as us?' Rachel asked.

'Oh, yes. I'm just not hungry.'

'What did you eat on your world? And what did you look like?'

'It's a long time ago, Rachel. It's not something I like to remember. I'm almost as human now as you or Theo. . . Do you think you can go on? You've done very well but there's still a great deal to get through.'

They had another session 'seeing' the stones. Rachel held hers steady for almost a minute. But Theo could manage only the same twelve seconds. He saw that Mr Jones was disappointed.

'I'm sorry.'

'Have a rest, Theo. You've had enough for a while. We'll concentrate on Rachel.'

'I can beat her. It's just that I keep wanting to know why. How it happens, I mean. There must be a scientific explanation.'

'I thought that might be it.' Mr Jones sighed. 'Well, I can't tell you. There are mysteries, that's all. Rachel doesn't look for answers. That's why she's nearly there. Just think of it as something like – birth. Or time.'

'I'll try,' Theo said. But he was beginning to feel defeated. Why weren't there answers? There had to be. Mysteries were all right in books and pictures but in real life there were always explanations. He began to be angry with Rachel, who was stroking her hair in a way that meant she was pleased with herself.

Mr Jones said, 'Watch for a little while. I'm going to get Rachel to pick up her stone. And stop looking so clever, Rachel. It's going to be a good deal worse than the dentist.'

'Oh,' Rachel said. Her face went a little pale. 'I think I'll go to the toilet first.'

She washed her hands, washed her face, and dried them on a towel that had *Belvedere Hotel* stencilled on it. She looked at this with pretended interest. She even giggled. He was a thief. But all this was an attempt to forget – oh why had he mentioned the dentist?

'Where did you get that towel?' she said when she was back in the kitchen.

'I travel a lot, Rachel. And I haven't any money.'

'Did you steal those bottles of Fanta too?'

Mr Jones laughed, not very heartily. 'I always pay in some way or other. Now come on, my dear. Don't try to put it off.'

'All right.' She sat down. She wished he would not look so sorry for her. 'Do I just pick it up?'

He nodded. 'Drop it if it hurts too much. And remember, the longer you hold it the cooler it will be next time.'

She brushed her fear away as though it were an insect: no need to be frightened of spiders or wasps – they could sting you but that was all. She picked up the stone, and although it burned like steam from a kettle she held it, she kept her hand clenched – she held it though a crying noise forced its way between her lips. 'Oh, please, somebody. Talk to me. Say something. I can hold it if somebody says something.'

'You're a brave girl –'

'Not that. Tell me a story. Anything. Please.'

'Beneath the spreading chestnut tree, the village blacksmith stands –'

'Oh shut up, Theo. Mr Jones, please . . .'

'What, my dear?'

'Those twins. Those other twins. Tell me about them.'

'It was so long ago.'

'Their names? What were their names?'

'Johan. Lenart.'

'Funny names.'

'They were Swedish.'

'Show me. Please.'

Tears were running down her face. The heat was not growing, but neither did it seem to be getting less. She was sure the skin was burning off her palm. 'I know you don't want to remember. But I want to know. So tell me. Or else I'll drop it. It's burning me up.'

Slowly a picture began to grow in her mind. It was grey, and she knew the lack of colour came from Mr Jones's reluctance. But slowly it began to take other tones. Two boys, both with red hair, dressed in old-fashioned clothes, were at a table sewing boots with leather thread. They were in a tiny room, dark, littered with scraps of leather. A man seemed to be shouting at them.

'Where is it?'

'Uppsala. In Sweden.'

'When?'

'Eighteen hundred and eleven.'

'Is the man their father?'

'They're orphans. He's their master. They're boot-making apprentices. He was cruel to them. I took them away.'

She saw another room, simply furnished with beds, a table, chairs. The two boys were sitting at the table with their eyes fixed on the stones. One of the stones was red. The boy – she knew his name was Johan – reached out and picked it up. He grimaced, but held it. Then he grinned.

'It's not so hot for him.'

'He's had more practice. I didn't have to hurry. The Wilberforces were far away.'

She saw a sailing ship then, with grey patched sails. It was running before a strong wind amongst islands covered with green bush.

'She's a whaler. I paid the captain to bring us to New Zealand – yes, with stolen money. He set us down there, in the Bay of Islands. We came the rest of the way on foot.'

She saw them camping by a stream. The boys were roasting wood pigeons over a fire. Each of them held his stone tightly in his fist. Mr Jones was a little way off, resting with his hands behind his head. Words began to echo in her mind – but the language was foreign. The boys laughed as though at a joke, and Johan tossed his stone in the air, one-handed, and caught it neatly. Rachel felt jealous. But she discovered her palm was burning less.

Mr Jones smiled, sadly she thought. 'It's all right now, Rachel. You've got past the worst. You can manage now.'

'But you mustn't stop. What happened?'

'I'd rather not tell you.'

'Oh, please. Don't treat me like a child.'

'You are a child, my dear.'

'I'm old enough to hold this stone.'

'You've got to tell us,' Theo's voice said. 'You can't just stop. We've got to know. If we're going to carry on.'

'Yes. I know it's sad for you. But we've got to see what happened.'

For a while there was greyness in her mind. The stone burned in her hand like a freshly boiled egg. Then slowly a picture took shape out of the gloom. It was another camp, by another stream. The boys were chopping with axes, shaping a log canoe. Their clothes were more ragged now. Each had a cloth bag tied around his neck. The stones were inside – she saw a glow of red through the cloth of Johan's bag.

'This is Deep Creek at Torbay,' said the voice in her mind. 'We lived there for almost a year. The Maoris brought us food. We made friends with them. They had never seen red

94

hair before. They would have taken us out to the island too—but we made our own canoe instead. There seemed to be no reason for hurry. The Wilberforces were still underground, hollowing out their chambers. I spied on them from time to time. There's no way they can keep me out. We made our canoe. We fished and we swam. And the boys hunted for birds. This is Johan.' They saw a boy of fourteen in tattered clothes and a belt of woven flax. His red hair fell to his waist. He was sitting cross-legged on the sand, playing a tune on a wooden flute. 'He made the flute. Listen.' The tune came clearly—a light, skipping, merry sound made of half a dozen notes. Then they saw a camp-fire and Johan playing once more—this time slowly, mournfully. 'He's remembering his homeland. Johan was a dreamer. A poet. Mysteries didn't upset him. Like you, Rachel. And Lenart—he was the scientist, the one who wanted explanations.'

They saw the second boy, freckle-faced, sturdy, with his red hair tied in a knot. He was throwing pipi shells into the wind, curving them first to the left, then to the right. 'He was the one who designed the canoe. See, he even made a sail of flax. And his stone—he never stopped peering into it, trying to see what made it work. It gave him a burn now and then when he got too cheeky.'

The picture faded. She saw a lean-to hut under the stars. The boys were sleeping on beds of fern. Mr Jones sat in the doorway, watching.

'I came to think of them as my sons. I didn't want it to end.'

The greyness came down on her mind again. It lasted a long time.

'Don't go on if you don't want to.'

But slowly a day dawned—sunny, cloudless, blue. She felt a breeze on her cheeks. The canoe was skimming along on the sea with its flax sail round as a melon and its outrigger lifting. Lenart was in the stern, using his paddle as a rudder, and Johan in the bow. Mr Jones was crouching by the mast, staring at Rangitoto straight ahead.

'Why there?' Theo's voice said.

'Because that's where the red stone must be used.'

The island came closer, grew taller. They saw its black reefs jutting into the sea. Johan had his stone clutched in his hand.

Abruptly the view changed. They were somewhere below the surface. Overhead the waves sparkled, undulated. The canoe cut through them, leaving a silver trail. And deep down, among the spines of petrified lava, something moved. At first it seemed a growth on a jutting stone. Then it detached itself and slid into the open. In shape it was between shark and stingray – in colour black and grey. They saw it passing their faces only a body's length away. Its thick tail drove it with threshing motions. It drove up towards the canoe, aiming for the centre of the hull.

The blow of its snout broke the canoe's back, lifted it clear of the water. The boys turned in the air in slow motion, flopping like broken dolls. They splashed down, yelling with terror, and Mr Jones, flickering now, turning into a figure of light, plunged towards the nearer – Lenart. He could save only one.

They saw Johan go down. The shark – the Wilberforce – had grown a bulbous limb and with this it held Johan's hair in a thick unbreakable grip. They went down, trailing bubbles, and vanished into a cave in the lava flow.

The red stone had dropped from Johan's hand. It sank with a gentle motion and settled among the anemones on the bed of the sea.

Greyness came down. The kitchen was utterly quiet. Large warm tears rolled down Rachel's cheeks. The stone in her hand had the warmth of blood.

*

By nightfall Theo could see the shape of his stone for almost half a minute at a time. He had tried holding it, had held it for as long as seven seconds. But the pain had been too great. He felt as if the skin were shrivelling on his palm. When he looked at it afterwards he was astonished to find it pink as ever, unblistered.

Rachel watched, pale-faced. She had spoken very little through the afternoon. The story of the Swedish twins throbbed in her mind. Mr Jones had recovered Johan's stone – the Wilberforces could not touch it. He had found his body floating in the sea. They buried it beside Deep Creek. Then he had taken Lenart back to Sweden. But the boy had lost all interest in life. He died on the journey.

'I'll hold this thing if it kills me,' Theo said.

'That's enough for today. I'll take you home now. You can get a good night's sleep and we'll try again tomorrow.'

'What if the Wilberforces come after us?'

'Lock all the doors. All the windows. I'll be outside. I'll be guarding you every minute.'

'Can I take my stone? Johan's stone?' Rachel asked.

Mr Jones went to his bedroom. He came back with two small bags made of a cloth like silk. They were white, threaded with draw-strings, one blue, one red. 'Wear them round your necks. They're yours now.'

They put the stones in the bags – Theo handling his like a hot potato. But when it lay against his chest it had only a faint warmth.

They walked home through the dusk with Mr Jones between them. Theo felt he was the old man's protector rather than the other way round.

The stone – Lenart's stone he had to think of it now – was warm against his breastbone. Tomorrow he would hold it. For the moment it was a companion. It made him less afraid.

8. IN TIME FOR THE PARTY

Aunt Noeline had left them a note on the dining-room table:

Dear Twins, Uncle and I have gone out to a bridge evening. We'll be home about midnight. Ricky will look after you. Don't stay up too late. Love, Auntie.

Across the bottom Ricky had scrawled: *Hey you kids, where in hell have you been? Couldn't wait. I've gone to pick up the gang. We're going to have a party. See you soon. Ricky.*

'That's great isn't it? Are you sure the doors are all locked?'

'I don't want a party, I want to sleep.'

They turned on the T.V. set and watched part of a programme. Neither of them could get interested.

'Did you see Mr Jones when that thing attacked? He turned into fire. Do you think he'll ever let us see his real shape?'

'He wants to be human. Just think how lonely he is.'

Theo got up and turned the T.V. off. 'I wonder why he hasn't told anyone. The army for instance. They could plant explosives down there. Blow those things sky-high.'

'It isn't the army's war.'

'Why? They're going to turn the Earth into mud.'

'It's the war of the Wilberforces and the Joneses. We're Joneses now, not Mathesons.'

'Honorary Joneses.' Theo warmed his hands an inch from his stone. 'I wonder how these things work. Do you think they explode?'

'No.'

'What then?'

'I don't know. Theo, have you thought, the Wilberforces are the last ones too? The last of their kind in the whole universe.'

'It serves them right.'

'No it doesn't. They're only doing what they have to do. I think – I think we should try to save them. Like the Notornis – and the blue whale. Otherwise they'll be extinct. We could give them a place to live – put a bog wall around them.'

Theo shook his head. 'You saw what they did to Johan. And remember that model under the lake, with the world turned into mud.'

'Yes.' As usual she could not answer him. But she felt she was right. Only when she remembered the smell – it was strong tonight – and the slugs sliding out of the cellar, and Johan, did she feel there was something evil about the Wilberforces. But pigs smelled, and hippopotamuses. Crocodiles, octopuses, snakes, worms, were ugly or slimy. Lions killed. Hawks killed. That didn't make them evil, simply different. She sat at the table worrying about this. Theo had gone to his bedroom with Uncle Clarry's binoculars.

'It's all quiet over there,' he called.

'All they are is different, Theo. Octopuses are different too.'

'Octopuses don't want to turn the world into mud. I'm going to do some practice with my stone. I'll see you in the morning.'

'Is Mr Jones out there?'

'I couldn't see him. But he'll be around somewhere. Don't worry.'

The doorbell rang. It rang with a long hard clangour, like a burglar alarm.

'Who?' they pebbled, staring wide-eyed.

'Ricky?'

'He wouldn't ring. Besides, there wasn't a car.'

'Mr Jones then?'

'He can just hop straight through.'

The bell rang again. Theo crept down the stairs and approached the door. Its wood suddenly seemed flimsy and the fastened safety-chain no stronger than a thread of wool.

'Do you think it's them?'

'I don't know.'

'I'm going to turn out the light.'

'No. They're better in the dark.'

'Theo, the smell, it's stronger.'

'You get back. Get in your bedroom and lock the door.'

'I'm staying with you.'

A heavy knocking sounded on the door, which vibrated under it.

'Let's try calling Mr Jones. Together.'

'What will we say?'

'S.O.S. Ready?'

They sent the message out – once, twice, three times. No answer came.

'He promised he wouldn't go away.'

The knocking sounded again and as it finished a voice called, 'Is there anybody home?' It seemed to belong to a young man. They sighed with relief. Theo went close to the door.

'Who's there?'

'Police. Open up.'

'What's the matter?'

'Is this the Cooper place?'

'Yes.'

'There's been an accident. I've got a message for the twins.'

There was something wrong about this and Theo began to be suspicious. But Rachel cried out, 'What is it? Is it our parents?'

'Yes. Your parents. They've been hurt.'

At once Rachel rushed to open the door. Theo caught her arm. 'Wait. Don't. There's something fishy.'

'Come on, young fellow. Don't fool about. Open the door.'

'We've been told to keep it locked. What's your name?'

'Brown. Constable Brown.'

'What's your number?'

'Seven four six two.'

'What sort of accident was it?'

There was a pause. Then the voice said, 'Their house burnt down.'

'Oh, Theo –'

'Keep quiet. Let me handle it. – Where is the house? Where do they live?'

He felt something slow, angular, wet, probing in his mind, and he thought desperately, Hamilton, Hamilton.

'Hamilton,' the voice said. 'Now come on with this door. I haven't got all night.'

'You're wrong,' Theo cried. 'It's Taumarunui. Our parents live in Taumarunui. Ring the police, Rachel. It's one of them.'

At once there was a heavy blow on the door. Theo flung himself against it. Another blow fell and then the door began to creak under a steady pressure. Timber began to crack around the lock.

'I can't find the number,' Rachel shrieked.

'One one one, you fool.'

The lock burst and the door jerked open the length of the safety-chain, knocking Theo off balance. He steadied himself and lunged forward. His weight made no difference. The door stayed a fraction open. A hand came sideways through and pressed down on the chain, trying to tear it off the wall.

Theo grabbed Uncle Clarry's binoculars from round his neck. He swung them on the end of their strap and brought them down on the hand with all his force. But they bounced off just as the camera had bounced off the baby slug in the tunnel.

Rachel was still fumbling with the telephone book. 'I still can't find it,' she shrieked.

'One one one.'

He rushed across the room to the telephone, picked it up, dialled one . . . The chain broke from the wall and the door slammed back with a force that shook the house.

It was indeed a policeman standing there. He lurched in: a young man, pink-faced, two metres tall or more.

'There's been an accident,' he said in a thick ugly voice and he advanced clumsily towards them. An overpowering smell moved along with him. The hand that had broken the chain was not a hand—it was shaped like a huge grey mitten.

'You're a Wilberforce,' Theo yelled. 'Keep away from us. We can burn you.'

'Come with me. Come to the lake. One will be enough.'

'Stay away.'

'You come. Or else I'll take your sister.'

The words were spoken with great effort. Theo remembered that keeping a human shape was tremendously hard for a Wilberforce. It took almost all their will, all their strength. Speech must use a good part of what was left.

'Up the steps, Rachel. Keep away from him. He can't move fast.'

They backed away and started to mount the steps. The Wilberforce walked after them slowly. By himself Theo would have risked ducking round him and making for the open door. But Rachel was no good at that sort of thing. She was bound to be caught. And getting caught meant being dragged to the lake and drowned. The Wilberforce spread his arms. They covered the whole width of the staircase. Heavily he started to climb. He had not troubled to re-form the hand that had broken the chain from the wall and this flexed in a livelier way, more naturally than the other. He face was calm – pink, young, handsome. He did not bother with speech again.

Theo and Rachel stood at the top of the steps and watched him come. There were ten steps, broad and shallow. He was hardly ten strides away, his head level with their knees.

Rachel grasped her stone. 'Make the light, Theo. The way we did before.'

At once their minds were together. Light, they thought, light, and the intense invisible beam sprang out, more easily, more powerfully than before. It struck the Wilberforce in the face. It hurt him, blinded him. He gave a quack of pain and recoiled as though he had walked into a wall. But then he stood his ground at the bottom of the staircase. His eyes sank deeper into his head. Their brown began to grow darker, turn into grey, into black. Their aperture narrowed to a slit. Then slowly, painfully, quacking with the effort, he began to advance again. He leaned forward as though against a huge weight.

'Harder,' Theo yelled. They increased the strength of the beam. It stopped the Wilberforce but did not drive him back. His face began to lose its pink colour and the fingers of his human hand run together. 'He's turning into a slug.' Theo fought to make the beam even stronger. But he felt himself beginning to falter. It was too much, he could not keep it up. He was on the point of blacking out. The Wilberforce stopped re-making himself. He moved up another step.

'I can't keep going, Rachel.'

'Try, Theo, try.'

'I can't.' But he joined in again and for a moment they held the Wilberforce where he was. Then he moved again, another step, against the full force of the beam.

'It's no good.'

'What are we going to do?'

'You go that way. Split up.'

They ran one each way along past the bedroom doors. 'Don't go in,' Theo yelled.

The Wilberforce climbed more easily. He reached the head of the stairs, looked at Theo first, then Rachel. He began to walk towards her.

Theo rushed at him. He gripped the material of his uniform jacket and tried to pull him off balance. But it was not material. It was the Wilberforce's skin, hanging loosely on the body underneath. It was damp and rubbery and slipped from Theo's grasp. He lost his balance and sat down heavily on the carpet. The Wilberforce turned. He made a lunge at Theo, but Theo scuttled sideways like a crab, keeping under the grabbing hands. He rolled frantically and jumped to his feet. The Wilberforce followed, then saw that Theo was out of reach. He turned to Rachel again.

Theo tore open the door of the storage cupboard between two of the bedrooms. He had found Uncle Clarry's golf clubs there in his exploring. He pulled one from the bag – a long wooden one numbered 2 on the leather bag protecting its head. He ripped the bag off and gripped the club near the top of its handle. It was dangerously heavy, and whippy as a piece of bamboo.

The Wilberforce had Rachel trapped against the wall beyond the farthest bedroom. She was holding him off with the light-beam, making it on her own with such force that he was even pushed a step or two back. But Theo could see her exhaustion. She could last only a moment or two more.

He ran at the Wilberforce, swung the club high and wide

and brought it down on the side of the creature's head. It bounced back with such force that Theo almost lost his grip on it. The Wilberforce stood steady as a rock. The skin of his face showed no effect from the blow. But he turned side on, seemed undecided what to do. Theo struck him again, a blow on the chest. And again the club bounced. The Wilberforce made up his mind. He turned back to Rachel. Theo attacked wildly. He struck the Wilberforce a dozen times – shoulders, head, neck, even legs. But only the helmet was damaged. It caved in a little and made a hollow sound. The Wilberforce quacked. He retracted the helmet on his head, made it a plate of rubbery skin.

Theo struck again, again. Rachel was pale as paper. Her strength was nearly gone. The Wilberforce inched forward.

Fire, thought Theo, matches. He dropped the club and ran down the steps, heading for the kitchen. But as he reached the lower level he saw a way Rachel might escape. He had chosen stupidly, going right at the top of the steps and sending her left. On the right the drop from the bed-room level was less than two metres. On the left it was three or more into the conversation pit where the floor was brick under the sheepskin rugs. But the built-in seats around the sides had cushions as fat as mattresses. If she could jump on to those . . .

He ran into the pit. 'Rachel,' he cried, yelling and peb-bling at once, 'jump. Climb the bannister and jump.'

He could not tell if she had heard. All her concentration was in the beam.

'Jump, jump,' he screamed.

She heard. She edged towards the bannister. The Wilber-force was released a little. He lurched forward. But she held him off again. She even pushed him back a step. She felt for the bannister, gripped it with her hand. And then she had to look away from him to lift herself over and he came at her in three great strides that made the floor shake. She did not jump, she simply pushed herself out and fell. His hands lunged, brushed the cloth of her blouse, but missed their grip. She fell sideways and landed heavily on the cushions, then rolled off on to the floor, tangling with Theo who had rushed forward in an effort to break her fall. He jumped to his feet and tried to pull her up but she was dazed. The Wilberforce had started back and was striding clumsily down the stairs. They were not going to make it. By the time he had her on her feet it was crossing the room to the stairs that led into the conversation pit.

'This way,' Theo yelled. He dragged her across the pit to the rail by the dining-room door. If they could climb that there was a chance of beating the Wilberforce to the front door or perhaps heading out through the kitchen and getting the back door open before he arrived. But he saw what Theo planned and stopped his advance. He moved across the room to a position that blocked both lines of exit. Then he began to come forward again. He would climb the rail himself, trap them in the pit.

Theo waited. It was going to be touch and go. There would be an instant when they might get away up the stairs again. He felt like a general planning a delicate manœuvre – except that here failure meant the lake.

He pebbled instructions to Rachel and heard her reply in a tired, dazed way. The Wilberforce reached the rail, gripped it, hefted his leg.

'Now. Go. Run.' He pushed her. She went across the pit, up the steps into the lounge, up the second set of steps, all at a tired run. Theo kept at her heels. If he had been alone he could have reached the open door without being caught. But he felt her exhaustion beating on his mind. She would not have been able to move fast enough. Making the beam of light had taken all the strength she had.

The Wilberforce had been caught by surprise. He moved again to block the door, but came to the steps more slowly.

They were now in the same position as before: the Wilberforce looking up, the twins looking down, the ten steps in between. But there would be no beam of light this time.

'You can't catch us,' Theo said. 'And you'd better get out. Mr Jones is coming.'

The Wilberforce seemed to do something with his mouth – re-make something inside it. 'Give me the girl. I'll let you go.'

'No,' Theo said.

'Push her down.'

'No.'

'I'll drown you both.' He spoke as though his tongue were a wooden clapper.

'You can't catch us,' Theo said. 'We'll go round and round like this all night.' He moved Rachel and himself a little to the right. 'If you try to come up we'll jump down and be out the door before you can get us.' But he knew Rachel would not be able to manage. Please come, Mr Jones, please come, he prayed.

The Wilberforce stood still for a moment. Then he moved with frightening speed, taking the steps three at a time. The twins reached the far end of the railing, climbed, Rachel in a drunken way, dangled their feet over, ready to jump. The Wilberforce stopped again at the head of the stairs. They were all three still.

'We've got you beaten,' Theo said. He tried to grin.

The Wilberforce's face turned grey. He moved again, faster than before, crouched like a skater.

'Jump,' Theo yelled. He threw himself forward, hit the floor, and rolled out on to the carpet. Rachel thudded behind him. But she did not roll. She knelt quickly, stood up, tried to run; and the Wilberforce bent his body over the rail, reached down with his huge arm, caught her by the wrist. He began to draw her up like a fish. She made no sound. She had a shocked agonized look in her eyes. Her face was soft,

107

white, shadowy, remote – a face that Theo no longer knew. It was as if she had already gone into another world.

He gave a cry, more of grief than rage, and threw himself forward in a rugby tackle. He caught her round the waist, tried to drag her down on to the floor. His weight made no difference. The Wilberforce raised them both as easily as he had raised the one. Theo felt the strain on Rachel's body. He let go and saw her drawn up out of his reach. The Wilberforce lifted her over the rail, still with one hand holding her wrist, and dropped her to his side. He could have killed her then, with a single blow – but his plan was made: the lake. He started for the steps, pulling her behind him. Theo met him halfway. He attacked with all his strength, with the ferocity of an animal, with fists, feet, knees, teeth. But the Wilberforce simply walked straight through him, tumbled him head over heels down the steps and shoved him away with his foot at the bottom. He walked on towards the door.

Halfway across the room he stopped. Theo, on his knees, saw and heard it too. Lights, engines, voices, laughter. He gave a cry and scrambled across to Rachel. She was trailing behind the Wilberforce like a doll. He lifted her, tried to break her free. The Wilberforce began to go forward again. Then people came through the door in an avalanche: Ricky, and five, ten, twenty, girls and young men carrying guitars, bongo drums, accordions, bottles of soft drink and beer.

The shouting and laughter stopped. They surrounded the twins and the Wilberforce. They stared at them with amazement.

The Wilberforce had been busy. He had re-made himself. His helmet was a peaked cap now. His pink face glowed with health. His eyes were cornflower blue. The hand that had been a mitten had five fingers which were locked about Rachel's wrist. He smiled.

'Excuse me. I'm taking this young lady down to the station.' His voice was firm, reasonable, perfect. Theo realized the tremendous effort it must be taking. While he kept this up the Wilberforce would be able to do little more than stand still.

'Don't let him, Ricky. He's going to kill her.'

'Easy on,' Ricky said. 'What's all this about?'

'He broke the safety chain. He chased us all over the house. And now he's going to drown her in the lake.'

Someone rattled the chain at the door. 'Hey, it's broken all right. Look at this.'

The Wilberforce still seemed unconcerned. 'Stand aside please. I'm only doing my duty.'

'Did you break that chain? You're a pretty funny cop.'

'I'm sorry, sir. We'll pay the damages of course.'

Theo began to be desperate. There was something hideously wrong about this. The Wilberforce was up to something. He was too patient.

'Ricky, he's not a cop. He's a monster. He comes from another planet.'

'Take it easy, kid. Now listen you – Mr Cop – what's the charge? Why do you want to take her down to the station?'

'We've had a complaint about shop-lifting. This young lady was seen . . .'

Theo became aware of a whisper in his mind, a thread of sound. It was so weak, so far away, he thought at first it came from the other side of the lake.'

'Theo. Theo. Help me.'

'Rachel?'

'He's killing me.'

'Rachel, wait. We won't let him take you.'

'My arm, Theo. My arm.'

Suddenly a girl shrieked, 'Look. Look at her arm. It's all gone grey.'

They all stared. The Wilberforce's hand, pink and plump, encircled Rachel's wrist firmly. Below it Rachel's hand was the colour of mud. Each of her fingers was curled like a dead caterpillar. Above, her arm was mottled white and grey. Theo put his hand on it. It felt like wet rubber.

'Theo, it's going into my shoulder,' the tiny voice whispered.

The Wilberforce smiled, more rigidly. His voice had a wooden sound. 'I'm only doing my duty.'

'Let her go,' Ricky said. 'You don't have to hold her that hard.'

'He's freezing her,' Theo cried. 'It'll get to her heart.' He tried to prise the Wilberforce's fingers up, but they felt like stone. 'Stop him. Ricky, please . . .'

'Come on, boys,' Ricky said. He jumped at the Wilberforce, recoiled with a shout of surprise at the rubbery feel of him, then launched himself again. His friends dropped their bottles and guitars and followed him. The Wilberforce heaved them off. He kept his grip on Rachel's wrist and started for the door. But the boys came back. They piled all over him. He bucked, heaved, ploughed ahead. Rachel was dragged after him, and Theo clutching her waist was dragged along too.

Suddenly Mr Jones was in the room. A high wild cry unlike any Theo had ever heard broke from his lips. He came forward in two light strides; he seemed not to touch the floor. The boys parted and even the Wilberforce fell back. Mr Jones's fingers sparked like electricity. They slid between Rachel's wrist and the Wilberforce's hand. There was a quick angry hiss and a small cloud of steam floated up. The Wilberforce, his face running into lumps, gave a quack of pain. He dropped Rachel's arm, but at the same moment swung a great blow at her with his other hand. Somehow Mr Jones blocked it. The fist slid off his body, shooting out sparks, and the Wilberforce quacked again. He lurched at Theo, his arms outstretched, but Theo ducked away. Mr Jones's voice rang in his head. 'Keep away from him, Theo. Keep behind the others.'

But the boys were not still. Shouting angrily, they threw themselves on the Wilberforce again and managed to wrestle him on the floor. He rose, throwing them off like sprats, but another dozen came at him. Theo and Rachel and Mr Jones were safe at the other end of the room. The Wilberforce looked at them for a moment. He peered at Rachel, limp in Mr Jones's arms, at her grey arm, slanting stiffly from her side like the dead branch of a tree, and his eyes, deep in his head, seemed to gleam with triumph. He gave a quack – a satisfied quack. He turned and ran out the door, bowling over a girl who stood in his way. The boys went after him like a pack of dogs. Their feet crackled on the concrete path. But louder still came a splashing sound from the lake, and their cries of surprise and disappointment echoed in the night.

'He's gone,' Theo said.

Mr Jones looked at Rachel. 'Come with me, Theo. Come quickly.'

He carried her up the stairs.

9. NARROW NECK

'Will she be all right?'

The old man made no answer. He laid her on her bed and lifted her dead arm carefully to her side. His face was white, smudged about the eyes with shock and grief. 'There's a chance,' he whispered.

One of the girls had followed them into the bedroom. 'Is there anything I can do? Shall I ring for a doctor?'

'A doctor can't cure this. Keep those others out. And keep them quiet.'

He ripped open the sleeve of Rachel's blouse. The grey had mounted almost to her shoulder. It crept upwards as Theo watched, at the pace of flowing treacle, and began to round the curve of her shoulder. It would be at her lungs and heart within minutes.

Mr Jones's hands flickered with light. He curved their fingers and gently fitted them in a band above Rachel's upper arm. A small piece of grey showed above them and crept on, a lengthening worm, making for the base of her throat where a pale blue artery pulsed. Mr Jones laid his finger along it, held it still. His hands were transparent, a pale golden colour, like apple-juice. Theo could feel warmth rising off them.

'Theo,' Mr Jones pebbled faintly.

'Yes?'

'Take out her stone.'

He loosened the draw-string of the bag about her neck, felt inside for the stone, and drew it out. She gave a faint moan and thrashed her head.

'Easy, child. No one's stealing it . . . Now, Theo, lock it in her hand. Force the fingers. Force them. We've got to get this coldness out.'

Her finger joints cracked as he bent them. His own fingers when he withdrew them were coated with a grey oily substance that quickly hardened and then crumbled into the same grey dust that had coated the floor of the Wilberforces' cellar. But the stone was locked in Rachel's hand. Moments passed. He saw the faintest tinge of pink advance into the grey.

He knelt at the side of the bed beside Mr Jones and watched the struggle go on. The stone itself would not be enough. It might bring the dying flesh of Rachel's hand back to life, cell by cell, but before that could be completed Rachel would be dead – the creeping coldness would have reached her heart. So everything depended on Mr Jones. And the old man was pale, shrunken, he seemed to be wasting away. His skin was the colour of milk and he seemed not to breathe. All his life, all his will, had passed into his hands. And they glowed, they danced with light, they radiated warmth, they seemed almost to hum like electric motors. Theo saw a flow of current within them, and knew that this was passing into Rachel and fighting to block the advance of the Wilberforce coldness.

He kept his breathing shallow. Outside the door was a murmur of voices, and down by the lake thin cries from the boys as they searched the shoreline. But in the room there was absolute quiet, absolute stillness, except in the old man's hands.

At last, after hours it seemed, he raised his index finger. The skin underneath was pink. He stirred and some of the life came back to his body.

'Theo.'

'Yes?'

'I want you to go and sleep.'

'But I want to help —'

'You can help by sleeping.'

'But —'

'Away, boy. Do as I say.'

'Shall I tell those people to go?'

'No. While they're here we're safe.'

'What if they do go then?'

'I'm not letting them. Now sleep. There's more to do than you know.'

Theo opened the door and went to his bedroom. The girls, a dozen or more, were sitting on the stairs, talking quietly. He saw that somehow Mr Jones had them under control. They smiled at him dreamily and yet with an odd determination. Outside the house the boys prowled, keeping watch. Theo felt safe, and grateful, and at once so heavy a tiredness fell on him that it was all he could do to stagger to his room and fall on his bed.

When he woke it was morning. He had neither moved nor dreamed. His mind felt wonderfully fresh. He knew at once that this was to be the most important day of his life.

A smell of cooking came up from the kitchen. He washed and hurried down. Ricky and three of his friends were frying bacon and eggs. They looked tired but grinned at him.

'You were great last night, kid,' Ricky said.

They sat at the table and ate.

'Where are the others?'

'Jonesy sent them home. There's just us four.'

'What about Uncle and Auntie?'

'They're sleeping. They were up keeping guard most of the night.'

'Is Rachel all right?'

'Sure. Sit down. Jonesy says there's nothing wrong with her.'

'Where's he?'

'He went out a while ago,' Ricky said. 'He left me in charge. I'll say one thing for that old guy, he tells you to do a thing and you go and do it.'

Theo finished his eggs. One of the boys brought him a cup of coffee.

'Did anything happen after I went to sleep?'

'We kept a watch, that's all. He didn't come back, that weirdo. He's either a good swimmer or he's down in the bottom of the lake.'

Theo felt his confidence begin to dissolve. The memory of the Wilberforce came back, trickling into his mind like dirty water. He put his hand on his stone and pulled it away hurriedly: still hot. How was he supposed to use it? – and when? He pushed his coffee away.

'I'm going to see Rachel.'

'Right,' Ricky said, 'I'll come too.'

They went up the stairs and let themselves into her room. She was awake. She looked calm, healthy, rested. Her arm was lying outside the blankets. It showed no sign of its freezing by the Wilberforce. Her stone lay in her half-open hand. She tightened her fingers on it as Theo approached.

'How do you feel?'

'All right.'

'Does your arm hurt?'

'No. It's warm.'

'Would you like a cup of coffee? Or tea?'

'Yes please. Tea.'

Ricky went to get it from the kitchen. Theo sat on the bed. 'Mr Jones saved your life.'

'I know. I guessed.'

'I'm brassed off with him though.'

'Why?'

'He was supposed to be keeping watch. And look what happened. Some sentry.'

They were talking, not pebbling, and when Theo tried to look into her mind he drew back in alarm. She was very weak: her mind was clear, still, fragile – not to be touched.

Ricky brought in her tea and put it on the bedside table. He patted Theo's shoulder. 'Come on. She needs more sleep.'

'Just a minute,' Rachel said. 'I want to tell him something.'

'Well, make it quick. I don't want Jonesy on my back.'

When the door had closed she said, 'Theo, can you hold your stone yet?'

'No.'

'Go and practise. You've got to do it today.'

'All right. Can you sleep again?'

'Yes. I don't want this tea. Promise you'll wake me when Mr Jones comes back.'

'I will.'

He went back to his room, sat cross-legged on his bed, and took the bag from round his neck. He tipped the stone on the blankets and set his watch beside it. The stone flickered, then took its seven-sided shape. Its colour, he told himself, was clearer today. And the shape – he saw it for thirty-five seconds first time, without even trying. Elated, he picked it up. But its heat was no less – it burned him like a blow-torch and he dropped it with a yell. He sucked his fingers, scowling.

'We're supposed to be on the same side.'

After that he practised seeing, with greater concentration, and in a calmer, less satisfied way. He went inside the stone, as Mr Jones had taught him, he looked out from inside and saw himself peering in. He held the shape for forty seconds, forty-five. An hour went by, two hours. He held the shape for fifty-four seconds.

116

I'm getting it, he thought. He rested, cleared his mind. Then he reached out his hand and picked up the stone. It burned, less badly than before, but enough to force a cry between his teeth. He held on. It did not build up, it kept its steady heat – and he knew that if he could endure it for ten seconds he could endure it for twenty, and if for twenty then forty, a minute, five minutes. It was tiredness that would beat him, not pain. Pain was nothing.

After five minutes he put the stone down carefully on the blankets. The pain stopped at once. He looked at his palm. It was pink, healthy, unmarked.

He lay back, delighted with himself; but then thought of the next time. He wasn't sure he could do it again. He closed his eyes and tears ran down his cheeks.

'Theo,' a voice said in his head.

'Yes?'

'You're doing well.'

'It hurts.'

'I know. But you're getting better at it all the time.'

'It's easy for you . . .' He opened his eyes and sat up. Mr Jones was standing inside the door. 'You don't have to get burned.'

'I'm sorry, Theo . . .'

'And anyway, where were you last night? Rachel nearly got killed. You were supposed to be keeping watch.'

The old man crossed the room and sat on the chair by the bed. He looked dejected.

'A lot happened last night. The Wilberforces were very clever, and I was careless. They tricked me – very easily.'

'What happened?'

'The worms are waking up. No – don't be scared. Two of the big ones woke last night – under Mount Eden and One Tree Hill. The rest have been out of the spell for some time, except the father. We still hold him. And until he's free none of the others can move. That's the way our spell works. We bound them as a seven, a family, and while the father worm is bound the others can't move.'

'How long . . .'

'He's close, Theo. Very close. A few days maybe. But possibly only an hour or two.'

'Will they come up?'

'No –'

'We can beat them. We can use atom bombs on them.'

'That might destroy them. Theo, but it would destroy your world too. They won't risk it though. They'll burrow into the earth. They'll go so deep you'll never be able to trace them. And down there they'll hollow out their caves. Huge factories. Huge breeding ponds. And one day, ten years maybe, maybe a hundred, they'll come up with weapons you've never dreamed of, and machines – hundreds of Wilberforces. Thousands. They'll turn your world into mud.'

Theo sat without moving, almost without breathing.

'Is this what you found out last night?'

'I found out how close they are. They let me see something was going on. They went to Mount Eden, all seven of them, and I followed. I saw the worm had woken. And then they went to One Tree Hill. After that the father started back for Rangitoto. I could only guess what that meant. I was so afraid I went on ahead – as he meant me to. The worm was still bound – only just. I waited for the father, to see what he would do. But he never came. It took me too long to understand.'

'He was back here.'

'Yes . . . I'm old, Theo. Very old. I'm making too many mistakes.'

'Where are they now? Do they think Rachel's dead?'

'They're not sure. They're watching. But they're not worried. They know they've almost won.'

'What are we going to do?'

'Rachel must sleep. She needs a whole day. And you've

got to practise. You've got to be able to hold the stone – it doesn't matter how much it hurts. As long as you don't let it go.'

'All right,' Theo said. 'I hold it. Then what?'

'Then we act. Tonight. We may be in time.'

'Act how?'

Mr Jones shook his head. 'Not yet. I'll tell you both together. Just learn to hold the stone. No. Later. You need your lunch. You need to be strong. First of all though we're going to convince the Wilberforces Rachel is dead. Then they might stop watching and we'll have a chance of taking them by surprise.'

He led Theo out of the bedroom and down into the sitting room. Ricky's friends were still there, sitting around talking quietly and strumming their guitars. Mr Jones took Theo on to the porch. In a moment a large black car turned into the drive.

'It's them.'

'No, Theo. It's real. A real hearse. They've come for Rachel's body.'

It came down the drive and stopped at the door. A man got out.

'Is he hypnotized?'

'Nothing deep. Just enough to make him forget all about it as soon as he's back on the road.'

Ricky and his friends came out. They helped the undertaker carry a coffin from the hearse into the sitting-room. Everybody stood around in an embarrassed way, waiting for time to pass. The undertaker seemed to be in a trance. He stared at his hands and cracked his finger joints. At the end of five minutes the boys carried the coffin out again, leaning a little away from it to make it appear heavy. They slid it into the hearse.

'Stop grinning, Theo. Look as if you're sad.'

He covered his face with his arms and leaned on the back

of the hearse. Mr Jones put a hand on his shoulder. 'Come on now, let me take you inside.'

Theo let himself be led away. The hearse crawled up the drive and on to the road. And Theo, looking sideways, thought he glimpsed the movement of a blind at one of the Wilberforces' windows.

'Do you think they're fooled?'

'I hope so. We've got to be quiet now. In mourning.'

At midday Uncle Clarry and Aunt Noeline got up. They had the same dreamy determined air the girls on the stairs had had the night before. Aunt Noeline made lunch. Then Theo practised with his stone again. It burned, but it burned a little less strongly. He put it down after five minutes, then after ten. There was no point in tiring himself. When he had to he would hold it, for as long as he must.

At three o'clock Mr Jones made him lie down. He slept and when he woke it was growing dark. His curtains were closed. Mr Jones was sitting in the chair and Rachel cross-legged on the end of his bed.

'Is it time?'

'Nearly. First you must eat. You'll need all the strength you've got.'

Ricky came in and turned on the light and Aunt Noeline brought in a tray loaded with plates of food.

The twins ate.

'How's your arm, Rachel?'

'It's fine.'

He saw she was holding her stone – Johan – and eating one-handed, and wondered if he should be doing the same.

'Is the big worm still tied up?'

'He was an hour ago,' Mr Jones said. 'We've got the rest of the night but no more than that.'

When they had finished he made them go to the toilet. 'Once we've started there'll be no time to stop.' The house was shadowy. Downstairs only the light in the conversation pit burned. Aunt Noeline and Uncle Clarry were there, talking in whispers with Ricky. His friends had gone.

'Now,' Mr Jones said, 'into the car.'

They went down the steps to the garage and climbed in the back seat of Uncle Clarry's Jaguar.

'Down on the floor.'

They crouched low and Mr Jones covered them with a blanket. 'Don't move until the car stops. I'll be waiting.'

'Where are we going?'

'Not far. Rachel, you're holding your stone?'

'Yes.'

'Theo?'

He fumbled it out and held it, grimacing. 'Yes.'

'It starts now. Don't let them go. Not for an instant. All right. Off.'

They heard the garage door rumble open. The car started and moved up the drive. Soon they heard the sound of horns and engines. Light filtered through the blanket. They were in Takapuna.

'Do you think we're going over the bridge?'

'Don't know.'

'Is your stone hurting?'

'Yes.'

They did not talk after that. They crouched low on the floor, feeling it vibrate under their knees. The car stopped three times at traffic lights. Uncle Clarry and Aunt Noeline talked softly and once Aunt Noeline reached over the back of her seat and rested her hand on the twins' heads in turn.

But Theo could bear his stone's burning no longer. Rachel was holding hers so easily. That was unfair. If they were a team the pain should be equal. Lenart was a red-hot ember, burning through his flesh, charring his bones. He had to have a rest from it. There might be hours to go. Surely, he thought, it would not matter if the stone rested on the floor for a moment or two.

He placed his clenched hand down beside his face and opened his fingers. The stone lay sandwiched between his palm and the carpet on the car floor. He drew his hand away. At once it was cool and he almost cried out with relief.

'Theo!'

'What?'

'My stone. It's starting to burn. Oh!' She opened her fingers. Johan fell out and lay on the floor, shining only an inch away from her eyes. 'Oh, Theo, I've done something awful.'

'Pick it up, quick.' He grabbed his own. It burned again, more fiercely. 'It's my fault. I let go first.'

'Mine's all right again. It's warm.'

'It's my fault. We've ruined the spell.'

'Oh, no.'

'Yes. He said not to let go. Not for an instant.'

'But we're holding them again.'

'It's no good. I know. It's ruined.' He clenched his hand more tightly, as if by enduring pain he could make up for his fault. But slowly the stone began to lose its heat. And Theo knew its life was going out. Don't die, he prayed, don't die.

The car crackled on to a shell road, and stopped.

'Out, kids,' Uncle Clarry said.

They threw the blanket off and climbed out on to the road. They were between street lamps, almost in darkness. A grass strip lay on their left alongside a sealed road. Beyond that was an open space that had the appearance of a golf course. On the right was a low concrete wall. The dark expanse of the sea lay beyond.

Mr Jones advanced out of the shadows. He waved the car away.

'There's a bench here. Come and sit down.' He stopped suddenly. 'What's the matter, Theo?'

'I let go my stone.'

Mr Jones stepped back as though he had been struck in

122

the face. He raised his hands. 'You fool, boy,' he cried. 'You fool. You've ruined everything.'

'I'm sorry.'

'Fool.'

Rachel jumped forward. 'Stop calling him that. It was hurting. I let mine go too.'

'Ruined. All the work of my people.'

He turned his back on the children and bowed his head. For a long time no one spoke. Then Rachel pebbled softly, 'What shall we do, Theo?'

'Who cares? Go home, I suppose.'

But Mr Jones's voice broke in. 'Come here. Follow me.'

He walked away, his head still bowed, and the twins trailed after him. They came to a seat in the deepest part of the shade between the lamps. Mr Jones sat down and the twins took places on either side.

'I'm sorry,' Theo said again.

'All right, boy. We tried. At least we tried.'

'Have I really spoiled it?'

'I think so.'

'What would have happened?'

'They'd have crumbled into dust. That's all.'

'The worms?'

'And the Wilberforces.'

'Can't we go on? I can hold it now. I thought it was going cold but it seems to have stopped.'

'It's lost most of its power.'

'But not all?'

'Who knows, Theo? I've got no way of telling.'

'It might still work.'

'Yes,' Rachel said. 'Mine seems to be talking to me. I can feel it pulling.'

'Where to?'

'Out there. Out to sea.'

'And yours, Theo?'

'No. It's warm, that's all. And throbbing a bit. As though it's hurt.'

Mr Jones was quiet. For a long time he sat without speaking. At last he said, 'We'll carry on. We'll place the stones. It can do no harm.'

'How do we do it? Where?'

'They're released over the father and over his leading son – over the worms. That means over the craters. We have to climb up and throw them in. That locks the whole family in the spell, the worms and the slugs – and then – well, they're supposed to turn into dust. But now . . .'

'Where? Which craters?'

'The red stone for the father. The blue stone for the son. That's the way we made them. There's no other way.'

'Which craters? Rangitoto?'

'When you release them each of you cries part of the incantation. It's simple to learn but it must be said. Rachel has the first part: "Go down, People of the Mud." And Theo: "We bring you the gift of oblivion." That's all.'

'I go to Rangitoto,' Rachel said.

'We go together. Rachel throws her stone first, over the father. And then we go to Mount Eden for the son. Theo does his part there.'

'But how do we travel?'

'Ricky's bringing the boat. He'll be here at exactly half past nine.'

'Where are we?'

'At Narrow Neck. Rangitoto's straight out there. You can see the light.'

They stared out to sea. Faintly they made out the line of hills on the Coromandel peninsula and the darker shape of Rangitoto in front. A small ship was moving past it showing half a dozen lights. The fixed light beyond was almost at the centre of the shoreline.

'We make for the southern end. The track goes up from there.'

'Won't the Wilberforces be guarding it?'

'I don't know, Rachel. If everything goes well they'll be down with their worms. Now, tell me what you do.'

'I throw Johan – I throw my stone into the crater.'

'And what do you say?'

'Go down, People of the Mud.'

'All right. Theo?'

'I throw mine. And I say: "We bring you the gift of oblivion." Don't you mean death?'

'Yes, death. We were more a race of poets than scientists. Now remember it. No more mistakes. And talk to your stone now. See if you can make it a little stronger. Ricky won't be long.'

Theo concentrated. He saw the blue gleam of the stone through his fingers. It coloured their flesh and made it semitransparent. He enjoyed its warmth and enjoyed its throbbing. It was wonderful, he thought, that this tiny piece of – whatever it was – should hold the whole life, no, half the life of a race. A race much greater and wiser than man could ever be. But that was a Rachel sort of thought: he put it aside. More to the point – had he ruined the thing? It was warm still, it had its seven-sided shape and its colour. The old man must be wrong. They'd turn those Wilberforces into dust all right.

Rachel was less happy. She stared at the shape of Rangitoto. It was so black, so threatening. A pale light was growing over its southern flank. The moon would soon be up. That did not make it seem any more friendly. She dreaded going there. She was troubled too by the thought that she was going to kill. The Wilberforces were the last of their kind. It was a crime.

'Mr Jones?'

'Yes, girl?'

'Couldn't we save them? Couldn't we talk to them?'

'No.'

'Isn't there another way?'

'No. Quiet now. I can feel something's wrong.' He stood up suddenly and stared over the golf course.

The twins stared too. In a moment Theo cried, 'There's Ricky.'

On the lighted road down the side of the course the beach buggy was speeding along drawing the trailer and boat. It looked like a toy – tiny and red and cheerful. It vanished behind a grove of trees.

'Down,' Mr Jones cried. 'On to the beach. Quickly.'

'Why? It's only Ricky.'

'Can't you smell them, boy?'

He pushed them along. And as they came to the boat-ramp they threw a last glance behind. A black car was speeding along the road towards the trees.

Their nostrils were suddenly full of the smell of the Wilberforces.

10. RANGITOTO

Ricky drove the buggy down the ramp and off the ledge at the bottom. It bounced a metre in the air and the boat and trailer bucked like a rodeo horse. He roared down to the water's edge, made a turn that threw up a sheet of sand, and backed the trailer into the water.

'They're following me. Get her off.'

Theo was already at the lock. He threw it open and worked the winch with his free hand. Rachel and Mr Jones hauled on the boat, one on either side. As soon as its stern was in the water Theo released the rope. Ricky shot the buggy forward and the trailer slid out from under the *Sea Lady*, leaving her afloat. He drove up the beach straight at the ramp and made a right-angle turn, blocking the bottom of it with the trailer. Then he started back down the sand.

'In you get,' he cried. 'They're nearly here.'

Rachel and Theo clambered over the sides while Mr Jones held the boat steady.

'Point her round,' Ricky yelled. The old man had her side on to the waves. He managed to turn her a little and Ricky, reaching his side, gave her a heave that brought her sluggishly bow-on.

'In. Quick.'

The Wilberforces' car turned into the ramp in a screeching high-speed turn. Its lights glared across the beach into the *Sea Lady*. Mr Jones vanished and appeared in the boat in the same instant. He grabbed Ricky's shirt and hauled him up.

The Wilberforces' car slowed a fraction, then surged forward again. It drove straight into the trailer, crushing it into the sand. A shriek of tearing metal filled the night. The lights went out. It seemed the car would stand up on its nose and topple over. But it ploughed forward, throwing up a wave of sand, before falling back on four wheels. Its engine roared like a truck's and shuddered free from the wreckage of the trailer. Straight at the boat it came, black and deadly, fast as a charging buffalo.

Ricky was on his feet, hauling on the engine-pull. The outboard coughed and failed to start. Again he pulled. The car was only a few metres from the water and the twins saw that the Wilberforces did not mean to stop. They were coming straight in, right to the stern of the boat. Ricky pulled. As the car wheels hit the water the outboard roared into life.

'Open her up.'

Theo jerked the throttle wide as Ricky leaped past him to the wheel. The boat sat up on its stern. But the car had plunged to within a body's length of them now, sending up a bow-wave that rolled into the boat. It checked her forward surge a moment. They saw Mr Wilberforce burst the windscreen open with a blow of his fist. He heaved himself through the shattered glass, scrambled along the bonnet, and launched himself head first at the *Sea Lady's* stern. One of his hands missed its grip but the other came down on an angle of the stern and found a hold. The boat pulled forward sluggishly. But now the car doors were open. The slugs were pouring out. One came after its father through the broken windscreen. They slid into the water with the speed of eels.

Theo had picked up the anchor as a weapon, but found it too heavy to swing one-handed. Mr Jones pushed in front of him.

'Keep back. It's you they're after.'

His hands turned into fire. He slid them under the Wilberforce's fingers and threw them off. The Wilberforce quacked with pain. At once the boat leaped forward, running like a greyhound out of a box. The slugs kept pace with it for a moment not more than a body's length away. The twins saw their circular mouths, their parrot beaks, the blunt knobs that served them as eyes. Then slowly they began to fall behind and before long the inky water showed no trace of them.

'Can we keep ahead?'

'I think so,' Ricky said. 'This thing can do forty.'

'Make for Rangitoto. Make for the light. We can't use the track now. We'll have to go up the hard way.'

The sea was dead calm. The boat sped over it like a skater on ice. Its hull vibrated faintly but only the bow-wave arching out on either side gave the twins a sense of speed.

'Can you turn off those lights?' Mr Jones said.

Ricky shook his head. 'It's against the law. We can't hide anyway. Look at the moon.'

Its rim had come over the flank of the island. It was coloured orange-red and the light it threw spread across the strait like the light of a flare. They saw other boats in it — yachts and motor boats cruising back from the gulf, a scow hauled by a launch, a coastal freighter waiting for its pilot — and far behind, but closer than they had expected, the small white foam patch made by the Wilberforces.

'They're on the surface. Keeping us in sight,' Mr Jones said. 'How far ahead can we get?'

'Maybe ten minutes. It only takes twenty to get there.'

The moon rose higher. Its lower edge cleared the island and its colour lost its richness. But as they sped on it seemed to fall. It touched the island again and sank into it as the *Sea Lady* came closer to the shore. They passed into blackness again. The sea was black as coal and now Ricky risked turning off the lights.

'Keep a lookout.' But he seemed to know exactly where he was going. A pale stretch of beach showed in the shore-line. He headed for it between two lava reefs and cut the motor just as Theo thought they were going to crash. The *Sea Lady* nosed gently on to the sand.

'Out,' whispered Mr Jones. 'Ricky, you get clear. Don't turn on your lights till you're well away. It's ten now. In about an hour you'll see a red light shine out of the crater. Be back here exactly an hour after that.'

'Right.'

'Be careful, Ricky,' Rachel whispered.

'You too. Good luck.' The boat chugged quietly out.

'Now follow me. We've got to get as far as we can before the moon lights up this side of the island.'

They hurried up the beach and into the stunted bush at its edge. The trees grew out of stone. Their trunks twisted and writhed and sometimes turned down towards their roots. Once properly in there, Theo thought, there was little chance of being found – and less of going fast. The crater might be only an hour away but it was going to take a lot of reaching. He stumbled on a rock and fell to his knees. He kept his hand closed tightly on his stone even though he felt skin tear off his knuckles.

'Now,' pebbled Mr Jones, 'I'm going to take control of you for a while. Just relax and walk as fast as you can. You won't fall and you won't bump into anything. Close your eyes if you like. I'll do the seeing for all of us.'

They obeyed – and Rachel did close her eyes. They walked as though they were on a street or beach. Occasionally they felt their sleeves brush against foliage. Occasionally they had to step high or long over a trunk or rock. But always their feet came down on level ground. Mr Jones walked ahead. His movements were those of a young man rather than an old one. Rachel felt the invisible rope that linked them. She closed her eyes again and walked with absolute confidence. Theo enjoyed it less. He felt as if he were in a fast car in heavy traffic – if the driver made a single mistake . . . And he puzzled about the scientific explanation. How was a thing like this done? Where were the rules?

'Stop now,' the voice commanded.

The moon was clear of the slope again and its light shone down the island, over the water, and over the city beyond.

'Keep low.'

'How far have we come?'

'Quiet. I want to listen.'

Faintly then, far away, they heard the quacking of the Wilberforces.

'They've landed.'

'Yes – they're working up. Coming fast.'

'Will they find us?'

'We've come around to one side. They'll go past us over there.'

'You mean they'll get to the top first?'

'Yes. They don't tire. They'll wait for us at the crater. They know they can't find us in this bush. They'll try to spot us coming up in the moonlight.'

'Can't they smell us the way we smell them?'

'Not unless they get really close. I'm taking you round to one side. They'll probably post themselves right round the crater. We'll find the weakest point and try to slip in there. But now we've got to go quietly.'

'Are you taking control again?'

'No, Rachel. I've got to save my strength. We've got a long way to go.'

She glimpsed his face in the moonlight and saw how weary it was – almost shrunken. It was the face of an old, old man – a dying man. He was killing himself to get them up this mountain. But she knew this was as it should be – she felt him give her the thought. If they failed he would have no reason to live any longer, and if they succeeded then his job was done. He would want the only rest he could know.

'Let's go on,' she whispered.

They climbed again, carefully, keeping low, keeping in the shade. Once Mr Jones made them stop and huddle on the ground, shielding the glow of their stones, while a Wilberforce went by only ten metres away. It crashed through the undergrowth like a wild boar, and made a sticky hissing sound as its body moved on the rocks. Its smell came strongly as though down a funnel. Further on it stopped and sent out its quack, once left, once right. Answering sounds came flatly through the night.

'What are they saying?'

'No sign of us, that's all. But they know they're ahead.'

Theo looked at his watch. It was half past ten. He could not believe they had been walking so long. But when he looked back he saw the land sloping endlessly to the sea. Ahead the peak of the island rose like a church steeple.

'How close are we?'

'It'll take another half hour. We're going to go round to the north. When we get on the rim I'm going to leave you hidden and go further round with Rachel.'

Theo nodded. It made sense. When Rachel had thrown her stone the Wilberforces would lose interest in her.

They climbed again, working to the left. At intervals the Wilberforces quacked to each other but the sounds became more distant and finally died away.

'They're at the rim. They're waiting.'

Every step now they made with care. Not a twig must crack or stone roll. Half an hour went by. A single quack sounded, close and to the left.

'Now I'm taking charge again,' Mr Jones pebbled. 'We've only got a hundred metres to go. Keep your stones well shielded.'

They moved silently through the stunted trees over ground that grew more level. Again Rachel closed her eyes.

132

She felt as if she were drifting off to sleep. Theo felt in the grip of a dream – a nightmare. He would rather have been left to shift for himself. The trees thickened. He had to twist, turn, duck, even crawl, to avoid rustling their leaves. His body felt as if it were doing a dance. He knew that if it did not stop soon he would try to break free. But Mr Jones halted at last. He released the twins.

'Now. We're right on the rim, in the thickest part of the bush. You can see down into the crater, Theo. There's a Wilberforce over there, right opposite. He looks like a big black rock. There's another one along to our left. One of the babies. Don't look, you can't see him. The mother's on our right about fifty metres away. Now, Theo. Stay here. Don't move, no matter what you see. I'll come back for you. Until then, not a sound. Don't even breathe. Rachel, follow me.'

'Goodbye, Theo.'

'Goodbye. Be careful.'

The words breathed in their minds. Theo wished they could have been spoken properly. But he kept still, kept quiet, did not even turn his head as Rachel and Mr Jones crept away. He was on his knees, crouching close to the ground, Lenart held tight against his chest. The opposite rim of the crater showed through a gap between trees. The Wilberforce over there had no shape. It was absolutely still. Moonlight gleamed on the oily slope of its back. Theo tried to see the rest of the seven. But only two other pieces of the rim were in his sight and these were clear. He closed his eyes and rested his forehead on the ground. Dreams of his home and parents and friends floated through his mind. That life seemed far away. He did not believe he would ever find his way back to it. Only the Wilberforces were real, and Mr Jones, and Rachel. The stone, Lenart, throbbing in his hand, was real. He wondered why oblivion should be called a gift. That was stupid – the Joneses must have been a stupid race. Oblivion was death, and death was horrible – and close.

Only a single mistake . . . He was struck with terror at the danger he was in. He curled himself up tighter, closed his eyes tighter, tried to sink into the ground. Please, he prayed, please, help me get out of this. I don't want to die.

A single quack sounded in the night. Heavy bodies crashed through the bush. He started up on his knees. But the Wilberforce on his right was heading around the back of the patch he was in. Across on the opposite rim the shape had gone from sight. And another was speeding over the rocks further round, its body gleaming in the moonlight. Theo saw Rachel. She was further on, well clear, standing in the light on the crater rim. She looked tiny. Beside her was Mr Jones – a small figure too, frail as an elf. The charging Wilberforce had the bulk of a rhinoceros. The two had no chance, and Theo began to move hopelessly to their aid.

Then he heard an echo in his mind: Mr Jones's voice, faint but sharp as glass. 'Throw, Rachel.' And he saw Rachel raise her arm obediently. The charging Wilberforce gave a frightened quack.

Rachel's voice rose into the night, clear, thin, careful, the sort of voice she might use for recitation. But to Theo it contained a note of grief. 'Go down, People of the Mud.' She drew back her arm and hurled her stone high in the air.

As it left her hand it turned a brilliant red, threw out spiky beams. The line of its flight was a perfect quarter circle, taking it unerringly to the centre of the crater. The force that propelled it was its own – Rachel could never have thrown so far. It lit the entire crater. The moonlight vanished. Nothing remained hidden. Theo saw sleeping insects on the leaves. He saw the round black mouth of the Wilberforce on the other side of the crater. But for the moment he was safe, for light of this sort would be darkness to the Wilberforces. Then the beams grew fuzzy, the flow lost its hardness.

'Down, Theo,' a voice said in his head. 'They'll get their sight back in a moment.'

'I'm all right.'

'Down, boy. It's you they're after now.'

He crouched again, but looked into the crater long enough to see the stone settle on the ground with the lightness of a butterfly and fade a little so that its light filling the bowl was a pulsating furry glow. After the spiky beams it seemed very weak.

Rachel and Mr Jones had gone. Across the crater the Wilberforce was moving quickly. Flat ugly quacking filled the night: the sound of creatures far from beaten yet. Branches cracked and stones rolled down the hillside with an iron sound. The hunt was on again.

Theo curled himself up tightly. He closed his eyes. Lenart throbbed in his hand. Its warmth now was less than the warmth of his blood.

11. WORM

A short way down the mountain Rachel crouched in the same position. But her hand was empty. Tears dripped from her cheeks. Gone. Johan was gone. Her hand seemed made of air – made of nothing.

'Don't be sad, Rachel,' Mr Jones said.

'I can't help it,' she sobbed.

'The stone was made for one purpose. It wasn't yours, my dear. It had a job to do and now it's done.'

'I know. Go and get Theo. Please.'

'Don't move from here.'

'I won't.'

'The Wilberforces have gone past now. They're heading down to the shore.'

'Please go away.'

He vanished. She sat up slowly and leaned back on a rock. After a while she put her empty hand into her armpit to bring it to life. Far away the Wilberforces made their farmyard sound. She was no longer scared of them, not for herself. But for Theo she was scared. They were going to guard the shoreline. And Mount Eden was so far away. Getting Theo there was impossible. How could Ricky bring the boat in while those things swam in the sea?

She stood up. The whole eastern side of the island was lit by the moon. The water had a greyish oily colour. On its far side the city glowed. She saw the curving line of lights that marked the bridge and the banked and clustered lights of the downtown area. Beyond was Mount Eden, a black hump topped with yellow beacons. It could have been on the other side of the world.

She freed her hand and held it in the air. It was warm now. Had it really held that stone? She was forgetting. Was that part of the magic? She turned and looked at the peak. A red glow fitted over it like a cap. That was real. Already boats would be starting out from the other side of the strait. Soon people would be up here. They would examine the stone, photograph it. Scientists would come. But they would never move it. Only when Theo placed his stone would it move, or vanish, or do what the Joneses had built it to do.

Only when Theo placed his stone . . .

She was filled with dread for him. The Wilberforces would never let him get off this island. They would hunt him like a rabbit.

'All right, Rachel.' Mr Jones was at her side.

'Where's Theo?'

'Waiting further down. Follow me. Be quick.'

They moved fast through trees and over frozen lava. Theo was waiting on the dark side of a huge overhanging rock.

'You were great, Rachel,' he pebbled. 'I hope I can do as well.'

'You will.'

'I didn't know you could throw like that.'

She saw Lenart glowing through his fingers and was jealous.

Mr Jones moved ahead impatiently. 'There's no time for chattering now. The hardest part comes next. Follow me. And be quiet.'

Once again they found themselves scrambling over boulders and squirming between branches and trunks. At first going down seemed easier than climbing up. They followed a shallow gully that kept them out of the moonlight.

Then Mr Jones turned to his right and led them through a tangle of bush that grew in deep crevices in the rock. Their hands and faces were scratched by twigs and stung by whipping branches. Theo, with only one hand, found it especially hard. Several times he fell and once scraped his shin so badly that blood ran into his sandshoe. He was puzzled that Mr Jones should lead them this way. Surely the beach where they had landed was round to the left. Even if the Wilberforces were waiting that was where they had to go.

'Aren't we going the wrong way?'

'We've got to keep clear of them.'

'But Ricky will be coming in. We've only got half an hour.'

'I know what I'm doing, Theo. Now let's keep going.'

They went on. The way became easier. Whenever they moved into moonlight Theo looked at his watch. Only twenty minutes left. Ten minutes. Five. The beach must be a good kilometre away. They were never going to make it.

Rachel too was growing anxious. She had no wish to face the Wilberforces again, but if Ricky had to they had to. She supposed Mr Jones had some plan for getting them into the boat. He would probably try to lure the Wilberforces away. But if Ricky brought the boat in before they were close it wasn't going to work.

They came to the shore. Mr Jones led them into a patch of shadow. 'Wait here. Don't move. There's a Wilberforce just along the shore.' He vanished.

'This is crazy,' Theo pebbled.

'I know. But we've got to trust him.'

'He's made too many mistakes already.'

'He's tired, Theo. I think he's going to die soon.'

They sat brooding about this. The smell of the Wilberforce along the shore was carried to them as though on a gentle breeze. Then Mr Jones was back at their side.

'All right. We'll rest.'

'Where have you been?'

'Talking to Ricky.'

'Where is he?'

'Can't you hear?'

They strained their ears and soon they heard the faint chugging of a motorboat. The *Sea Lady* came round the reef into the moonlight. It was moving slowly and Ricky was sitting in the stern as though out for an evening cruise.

'Is he coming in here?'

'He's going to the beach.'

'Why not here?'

'They'd be on us before we could get near the boat. He's going to wait for us at the beach. And so are the Wilberforces. You can hear our friend moving now.' A faint movement of a heavy body sounded below the noise of the motor. Theo began to understand.

'He's a decoy.'

'Yes, Theo. He's going to wait. And the Wilberforces are going to wait. And while that's going on we'll be heading for Mount Eden.'

'How?'

But Rachel broke in. 'It's dangerous for Ricky. Won't they attack him? They'll sink the boat anyway.'

'I don't think so. They'll lie quiet and try to catch us when we get there. They're not interested in Ricky. Now Rachel, there's one more thing. Theo and I will move faster by ourselves. I want you to wait for us here. We'll come back for you as soon as we can.'

She had thought this might be coming. Her body seemed to grow cold. Alone on this island with the Wilberforces . . .

'They won't touch you, my dear. Even if they find you. Theo's the one they're after now. And he'll be safer if we don't have you to slow us down.'

She saw the sense of it – but could not say yes. Alone with the Wilberforces. It was more than she could do.

Theo stepped forward suddenly. 'She's not staying here,' he said.

'Now, Theo – '

'I'm not leaving her here with those things.'

'You'll do as I say, Theo.'

'I won't. I'm tired of being shoved around. First the Wilberforces and now the Joneses. Well, I've got the stone and I'm telling you this, I'm not going to move unless Rachel comes too.'

'Please, Theo, I don't mind,' Rachel said.

'You keep out of it. He's getting too bossy. We're going together or we're not going at all.'

Mr Jones turned away. He walked a few steps and sat down in the deepest part of the shadow. The sound of Ricky's boat died away round the reef. At last Mr Jones said, 'All right, Theo. You're right, of course. It's your world, not mine. And your battle. I'll take you both. It'll slow us down but you must be together at the end – whatever it's going to be. Now let me get my strength.'

They were quiet. Theo grew ashamed of his outburst but felt a little better when Rachel pebbled softly, 'Thank you.'

'Do you think he's all right?'

'He's tired. He's dying, Theo. Be kind to him.'

Mr Jones stood up. He came to them and took them by the hands. 'Now for the last part, children. It's hard but you must be brave – and trust me. Rachel?'

'Yes.'

'And you, Theo?'

'Yes.'

'Guard your stone.'

'I will.'

'Then follow me.'

He led them through the shadows until they came to the sea. 'Softly. No splashing.' He walked in and they followed.

140

Rachel began to understand. She did not know whether she could go through with it. Perhaps it would have been better to stay behind.

They swam carefully, making no noise. In a moment they came out of the shadows onto moonlit water. At once she felt as if the Wilberforces' eyes were on her, that something was rushing up from below and she curled up her legs defensively. But Mr Jones kept steadily on and Theo, coming behind, gave her a push. She dog-paddled with care.

They were well out from the shore when the old man stopped.

'We're over it now. You first, Theo. I'll guide you down.'

'How far?'

'Just a short way. Hold your breath. I'll help you.'

They sank and Rachel was alone. A long time seemed to pass. The moon was so bright she felt as if a searchlight were playing on her. Surely the Wilberforces were coming. Surely that was a quack, a splash in the water. But nothing came. When Mr Jones appeared beside her she almost screamed.

'Easy, my dear. Take a deep breath.'

'Is Theo safe?'

'He's waiting for us. Just let yourself sink.'

They went down. She felt his hands pressing on her shoulders and when she opened her eyes she saw him glowing faintly in the water. Her feet touched something: a rock. She shifted them, felt about until they found something soft. The pressure came on her shoulders again. The jelly substance of the valve came over her ankles, over her knees, up over her body. Then she felt her legs come free and that made it more bearable when her face went in. At the last moment she clamped her hands over her mouth and nose. Then she fell and bruised her knees. But Theo was there, grabbing her, and Mr Jones came down lightly at her side.

She let out her breath and drew in another and the stench of the Wilberforces struck her like a blow.

'The father was down here only ten minutes ago, checking on his worm.'

'Is it free?'

'It will be before morning, Theo. Unless we place your stone. And unless it works. Now I'm going to give you some light. And then we'll slide. It's a long way down but there's nothing on the way that can hurt you.'

Quickly his hands appeared out of the darkness, at first as a pale yellow shape, then as a red-orange glow that lit the tunnel. The tunnel was similar to the one under the lake – the same height and roundness, the same walls of grey glassy stone.

'You first, Theo.'

Theo clutched Lenart to his chest and went forward to the point where the tunnel began its downward slope. Rachel followed. She saw him sit, glance back a moment, pale-faced, then push himself off. He vanished round the curve.

'Now you. Quickly.'

She sat and pushed herself forward. At once she was sliding at the speed of a sledge on a hillside. The force of her motion pushed her on to her back. She felt the tight cork-screw turns of the tunnel. Ahead was a swishing sound. That must be Theo. She could not hear Mr Jones but the light that kept pace with her meant he was following. The walls hurtled by, flickering with giant shadows. She shut her eyes and concentrated on keeping her legs and arms from flying about. If the tunnel did not level out soon she felt she would leave them behind. But on and on it went. How deep were they now? Much deeper than the bed of the sea, deep under the island. They must be almost down to the molten lava. As soon as she thought this she felt the air growing warmer and she almost screamed with fear. What would happen if the tunnel ended in lava? But then the twisting stopped and the slope began gradually to level out. Her speed dropped little by little. She opened her eyes. Ahead was a dark shape rushing onwards at the same speed as herself. That must be Theo.

Mr Jones's voice was in her head. 'This goes on right under the island. So just relax.'

She lay back and tried to obey. She closed her eyes. It was like being in a train – an underground train. Or in one of those tubes that delivered money and dockets in old-fashioned department stores. She would have enjoyed it if the smell of the Wilberforces had not been so strong. It was growing: it was so thick now she could feel it curling round her like steam. She tried to ignore it. Was Ricky safe? she wondered. How long before the Wilberforces realized they had been tricked? And what would Aunt Noeline and Uncle Clarry be thinking? She remembered her parents then. She thought of them reading the paper by the fire, working side by side in the milking-shed, drinking bottles of beer in the sun. Would she ever see them again?

The Wilberforce smell grew stronger. She could almost see it, yellow-green, like bad water in an old forgotten can.

Suddenly they burst into the open. She heard Theo yell. Her eyes were filled with red light. She was sliding through dust on a level floor. Then her feet struck Theo in the back and shot him forward. In another few metres he came to a stop and she slid along his side. Her legs plunged into something cold as snow. Whatever it was it felt horrible: cold, sticky, filthy. Theo yelled again, this time with disgust. He scrambled backwards, half running, half crawling. She followed in the same way, her hands plunging wrist-deep in dust, until Mr Jones caught her shoulder with one of his glowing hands.

'Calm down. There's nothing to harm you.'

'My legs.' They were coated with slime.

'It's mud, that's all. You both went into the mud pond. It's nasty but it won't do you any harm.'

His hand was warm and as he kept his grip she felt the iciness go out of her legs.

'It's like porridge,' Theo said. 'Where are we?'

'In one of their halls.'

They looked about them. The light came from a single clear red beam descending from a rocky ceiling high above them. As Rachel looked she understood its source.

'That comes from Johan.'

'Yes, Rachel. Straight down through the rock.'

It struck the rounded top of a cliff that rose out of the mud a hundred metres or more away, and there it disappeared. Rachel stared. The chamber was huge, it stretched away into the distance over the clifftop. It was larger, she thought, than any cave ever discovered or any hall ever built and she was filled with awe that it had been hollowed out by living creatures. It was large enough to house a warship or a giant tanker. But it was not for that. Somewhere up there on that huge black cliff was the worm that had built this place: a mindless body waiting for its brain. Waiting for its Wilberforce. It was held in the original spell, still held, by some tiny cluster of its cells, perhaps no more than would go to make one of her toe-nails. But held, all the same, till morning. And now it was pierced by the beam of light from Johan. She felt a great fear, but at the same time a dreadful desire to see it.

Theo too was staring ahead. He had scraped a handful of mud from his leg, looked at it closely, sniffed it, shivered, and tossed it away. This was the food of the worms, the mud they filtered their minerals from. And that meant . . . He fell back a step. He felt as if he were being steadily crushed into the ground.

'Theo,' Rachel whispered.

'What?'

'Where's the worm? Is he on top of that cliff?'

'No.'

'Where is he?'

He looked at her, almost with pity. He made himself believe. What other explanation could there be? He put his arm round her shoulders.

'You're looking at him, Rachel.'

'You mean . . .?'

'What you thought was a cliff.'

'Oh, no. No.'

'He's bigger than we thought.' He was whispering now. And the light-beam shrank for both of them, Johan's beam, until it seemed as thin as a cotton thread, more useless than a pin.

12. THE END OF THE WAR

Half an hour later they were standing at the entrance of
another tunnel. Mr Jones had left them for a moment to see
if the Wilberforces were still watching Ricky. The huge
cavern was silent except for the dripping of water from its
ceiling. They were head-on to the worm now. Its shape was
a half-circle, huge and black. Though the creature was blind
it gave the impression of watching them with a single pink
eye set in its snout just above the level of the mud. This was
the hole the Wilberforce would fit into when the monster
was freed.

Theo shivered. He hoped Mr Jones would not be long. If
the worm rolled over or even moved its head it would send
up a wave of mud that would smother them. He tried to keep
up his courage by doing mathematics. The worm was not
quite half a kilometre long (he had counted his steps as they
ran along the narrow shelf of rock between the wall and the
mud). That made it less than the size of a super-tanker. But it
was solid so it probably weighed more. It was segmented
like a garden worm but it had scales as well, each as big as a
dustbin lid. They had passed several lying in the dust but
when he had tried to move one it had budged only a fraction.
That must make it heavy as lead – heavier. He saw how an
army of these could turn the world into mud. No wonder the
mountain's erupting hadn't damaged it. He tightened his

hand on Lenart. It pulsed feebly, but its warmth was less than his own – and he was frozen.

Rachel stared at the beam of light. It was all that stopped her from screaming. It pierced the worm like a needle. She had done that. But the thing was so huge. Just the sight of it seemed to push her back against the wall, flatten her thin as paper. The tunnel was only a few steps away. If Mr Jones did not come soon she was going down – anything rather than stay here.

'Where is he?'

'He'll come.'

'The Wilberforces must have got him.'

'No. Where do you think this tunnel goes?'

'I don't care. I'm going down.'

'Hold on. Wait. He's got to come soon.'

'Oh Theo, I'm scared it's going to wake up.'

'Even if it did, it's blind.'

'It's watching me. I know.'

'Bullswool. Hey Rachel, look at that light from Johan. It's got him fair through the middle. Like a spear.'

They crouched in the mouth of the tunnel, shivering, waiting. Suddenly Mr Jones was at their side.

'All right. We can go now.'

'Why were you so long?'

'Easy, Rachel. I tried to lead them away, that's all. Now come on, we don't have much time.'

'Away from what?' Theo said.

'They were coming this way.'

'But why? What about Ricky?'

'It's all right –'

'What have they done to Ricky?'

'Rachel, I'm sorry . . .'

'Oh, tell me, please.'

Mr Jones took her hand. 'I think he must have lost his nerve, Rachel. I'm sorry. He was very brave – but being that close to the Wilberforces . . . He must have tried to get away in the boat and they followed it and smashed it before he could get up speed.'

'But Ricky? What happened?'

'He's – gone, Rachel.'

'Do you mean dead?'

'My dear . . . I'd hoped, I'd hoped so much . . . there'd be no more after Johan and Lenart.'

'Drowned,' she wailed. 'Oh, Ricky.' She seemed to be in the right place, down here in the cold, under the earth. She felt Theo's mind on her own, trying to comfort her, and saw how angry, how determined he had become. But none of it helped. She wanted to sit here and weep and never move.

Theo and Mr Jones got her into the tunnel. She lay down and felt them start her moving. Then for hours it seemed the walls slipped by in a blur made more by her tears than by her speed. In fact the tunnel had a shallow slope and only its smoothness kept them moving. Now and then Theo bumped into her from behind and she felt the pressure of his feet on her shoulders. More time went by. She looked about her and wondered if she had been sleeping. 'Oh, Ricky,' she sobbed.

Then the tunnel flattened out and she felt her motion stop. Theo slid to a halt beside her. He stood up and helped her to her feet. 'Where are we now?' she heard him ask.

'Under the harbour. This is as deep as we go. You'll have to walk from here.'

'What's this room?'

She looked about her. They were in another chamber but the only light here came from Mr Jones's hands and it barely reached the walls. Dark patches in the gloom marked the entrances of other tunnels. She took this in without fear or curiosity. Her mind was not working now. It held one picture only – of Ricky floating face down in a sea as black as oil.

'Where do these tunnels lead?' Theo asked.

'This is the terminus. They all meet here. That one comes from the lake. And Mount Wellington over there. Mount Eden's straight ahead, and One Tree Hill. Now come on. It won't be long before they think of looking down here. Your footsteps are all through the dust up in the worm-chamber. So we can't hide. We've got to stay ahead. You go first. If Rachel sees you it might help her keep going.'

Theo went into the tunnel ahead, pulling Rachel after him by the hand. He lowered his head to keep it from brushing the ceiling and started to run with an easy loping stride. Rachel dropped a little behind, but she would keep up, he knew. She was good at running. The glow from Mr Jones's hands lit the sides of the tunnel and cast a giant shadow down its middle. It was enough, there were no obstacles. Only the curve of the floor caught his feet at times and threatened to twist his ankles. He dropped his speed a little and glanced behind. Rachel was close to his back. The light shone through her hair but her face was in darkness. His grief was less than hers. Anger drove him on—anger with Mr Jones for getting Ricky killed and anger with the Wilberforces for killing him. There was nothing to do about Mr Jones – he was on their side. But at least he could get back at the Wilberforces. He was going to turn them into dust.

His neck and shoulders began to ache from bending. He slowed a little more.

'Walk, Theo,' came Mr Jones's voice. 'You can't keep up that speed.'

Unexpectedly, Rachel said, 'I can keep going.'

'So can I. Are you all right now?'

'Yes. We've got to get there.'

They kept on running. Rachel felt little tiredness in her body, but her mind was tired almost to the point of collapse. She knew she needed to sleep – sleep for days, bury the things that had happened on this holiday so deep they would never come back in their proper shapes. But first there was something that had to be done. Ricky was dead. And the Wilberforces who had killed him had to be turned into dust. Theo had to get to the crater. He had to get his stone into the crater. Ricky. Ricky dead. The Wilberforces. The Wilberforces alive. The thoughts followed one another like left foot and right.

The tunnel began to climb. They kept up their steady pace. Theo guessed they were somewhere near the point where the sea met the land, perhaps under the wharves. He wondered how they would get into the open again. He would have given anything to have been able to stand up straight.

At last they had to slow to a walk. Mr Jones came close behind them. His voice filled their minds. 'You've done well. I think we're going to make it.'

'Run, Theo,' Rachel said.

'What?'

'They're coming. I can hear them.'

But Mr Jones's hands were on their shoulders, holding them still. They crouched. And far away they heard a sound like the rushing of water from a tap in a room at the other end of a house.

'It's them.'

'They're coming down the slope. They've just come out of the worm-chamber.'

'That's the air we can hear,' Theo said. 'They're pushing it ahead of them.' And they felt a breeze lift their hair. With it came the smell.

'Run, Theo, run.'

Their horror of the Wilberforces overwhelmed them again, yet they ran with determination as much as fear, with a grimness and anger that drove them on to a goal. The sound of the Wilberforces coming down the tunnel increased until it was like a stream in flood. The breeze grew stronger. Suddenly it became a rushing wind that stretched their hair in front of them. The Wilberforces had crossed the terminal chamber and entered the tunnel climbing to Mount Eden. They were no more than a minute or two behind and coming with the speed of an express train. But the twins' own part of the tunnel levelled out. They sensed hollowness in front and a moment later burst into the open. They thought they were on the surface and the lack of stars and lack of a moon struck them with terror. Then the glow from Mr Jones's hands showed them walls of rock. They were in another chamber: the worm-chamber under Mount Eden.

'Keep going. This way.'

Mr Jones went ahead, trailing light behind him. They sped along a sloping ledge of rock. Far below, deep in a muddy basin, lay the worm. They saw it dimly, fleetingly. It had the appearance of an overturned battleship floating on the sea. The hole left by its Wilberforce made a pale mark on the black of its hide.

They ran shoulder to shoulder. Their feet made dead padding sounds in the dust. Mr Jones moved in a series of instantaneous leaps, vanishing each time they reached his side. The light from his hands grew dim then slowly increased.

'How far?'

'Just a short way.'

They saw the dark shape of another tunnel in the wall of rock. But if this corkscrewed up to the surface they were lost. They would never climb it. The thought came to them both in the same instant – and a second later came the hissing slithering sound of the Wilberforces bursting into the open. One, two, three. The giant males. A single flat triumphant quack echoed in the chamber.

'In you go. Quick.'

They crouched, went into the tunnel – and stopped, for

after a dozen steps it climbed and began to turn. Their feet found no grip on its glassy surface.

'We can't –'

'Stand still. Do nothing. I'm going to take you up.'

And he changed into his natural shape: he became a huge golden-red flame that burned and flickered from the entrance of the tunnel up to the place where they waited.

It advanced steadily, flowed over them with a warm gentle pressure, swallowed them. They caught hold of each other, saw each other through a golden haze that made Rachel think of honey, of nectar, of bees. And there was a faint humming sound, a hive sound, in her ears. She was not frightened. She smiled. She almost felt as if she were in bed, sleeping peacefully, dreaming.

'Be still, children.' The voice was in their heads, cool, remote, alien, and gentle. They began to move. Through the light they saw the walls slide by. Rachel found no way of estimating their speed. But Theo set himself to mark the turns. If this tunnel was made on the same plan as the one under Rangitoto he should be able to work out how fast they were going. And in a moment he knew it was not fast enough – not more than an easy running pace. The Wilberforces would be able to do better. They had built the tunnel to suit their style of moving. So everything depended on how close to the surface they were.

Rachel caught his fear. She turned her head and looked back. Through the golden light she watched the walls of the tunnel turn away and disappear. At any moment she expected to see the snout of a Wilberforce grow forward from the vanishing point. The creatures were in the tunnel now – they must be. And through the thin substance of Mr Jones's body she imagined she felt the rushing wind of their coming and smelt their smell.

The body jerked, and went on.

'Easy, my children.' His voice was straining now, its remoteness gone. And Rachel knew that Mr Jones had saved himself for this climb. He was pouring the last of his strength, the very last strength of his people, into it. After this he would be able to do no more.

'They can't catch us,' Theo said. 'Not in the tunnel at least.'

'Why?'

'They're pushing us along. The wind – the pressure. We're going faster. Can't you feel it?'

'But when we get to the top –'

'It'll blow the valve out like a cork from a bottle.'

A gentle, tired voice sounded in their heads: 'Theo the scientist.'

They turned, they climbed.

'How far back are they, Mr Jones?'

'Not far. Are you ready?'

'Yes.'

'Goodbye, my son.'

They were suddenly hurtled round. A roaring filled their ears. The moon spun crazily in a red-gold haze. The flame-body twisted sideways out of the savage wind released from the tunnel and settled on the slope like a butterfly. It vanished. Rachel and Theo lay side by side on a bank of grass. Beside them was Mr Jones, moving with an agonizing slowness. 'Away, boy,' came his voice, so feeble it was no more than a whisper in Theo's head.

He ran. Clasping Lenart, he ran.

'What can we do?' Rachel asked.

'Pray for him.'

The Wilberforces erupted from the hole in a whistle of air. The earth seemed to spit them out. Their speed was so great, the force of the wind from the tunnel so powerful, they shot high into the air and tumbled down the side of the mountain. But it took them only a moment to grip. They turned and charged back with the speed of wild boars.

Mr Jones had struggled to his feet. He tried to block them with raised hands that gave a ghostly flicker, but the leading Wilberforce brushed him aside without the slightest movement from its course and sent him tumbling head over heels down the slope. The two smaller ones were a dozen body lengths behind. Rachel faced them. She tried to make a beam of light with her mind but her strength too was gone and the creatures rushed by, one on either side of her, with unslackened speed. She flung out her hands and felt them hurled back as though by a jolt of electricity.

'Rachel, help me,' came the old man's voice. She scrambled down the slope.

'Help me up. I must see the end.'

She brought him to his feet, put her arm around him. Together they began to climb up to the crater.

Ahead Theo half-ran, half-scrambled, like a chimpanzee. He had his bearings now. The tunnel had come out on the south-western slope of the mountain a third of the way from its base. A grove of trees was on his left and bare grassy slopes on his right. Below and spreading far away were the lights of suburban streets. He threw quick glances behind him trying to see the Wilberforces and caught a glimpse of a black shape hurtling between tree-shadows. They were coming – coming at a speed three times his own. He ran, scrambled, skinning his knuckles and knees. Cattle lumbered out of his way, too slowly. He had to swerve. The coarse grass and the heads of flowering weeds wrapped themselves about his legs as though trying to hold him back. Then he heard a quack. They had seen him. He heard the rushing of wet heavy bodies.

Just in time he saw a fence. He vaulted over it, ripping his legs on the barbs of wire, and stumbled across an asphalt road. A bank next, crumbling clay. Up that. And over the Maori terraces – four of them. He heard the fence smash down, heard one, two, three bodies jangle through the wire.

But now there was only one terrace to go. The light of his stone grew stronger. He risked a look behind. The father was on the second terrace, the two sons on the first. They went from sight to mount the banks. Too close. Theo gave a cry of rage and despair. He hurled himself at the bank. He clawed with his fingers, scraped with the fist holding Lenart. And the top was under his hand. He stood on it, caught his balance. The crater, the city, the harbour lay in front – and Rangitoto capped with red. But the father was on the final bank, surging up, quacking with a heavy enraged sound.

Theo jumped. His feet slapped on the asphalt surface of the parking lot. It was wider than he remembered, as wide as a motorway. He was scarcely a quarter way over when the Wilberforce smacked heavily down behind him and hissed into full speed again. He ran as though the ground were falling away behind him. He raised his arm ready to throw. But that brought the Wilberforce on with a final rush that would take him before he could shout his part of the incantation. He swerved and the creature went by almost touching his heels. He ran at an angle towards the crater lip and the Wilberforce turned with no loss of speed and went with him, a little behind, rushing to block and catch him at the same instant. Three metres. Another three metres. But the Wilberforce was there and he had to swerve again. The creature had learned. It had grown a whip-like arm and as it swept by its tip found Theo's ankle and wrapped around it. Theo crashed down. He was dragged across the asphalt. He was stunned, scraped raw on his legs and elbows. But his grip on Lenart held. And as the Wilberforce turned to crush him he lifted his arm, gave a flick of his wrist, and sent the stone skimming away across the creature's back.

'We bring you the gift of . . .' he cried. And the final word was nearly lost. Why didn't they say death when they meant it? '. . . oblivion.'

The Wilberforce stopped. He could feel the coldness from

its skin. Its round mouth faced him like a tunnel. And from it came a single, lost, despairing quack.

The stone was climbing lazily in its flight, sending out blinding shafts of blue light. It hovered over the centre of the crater before it began to drop. The bowl was filled with light. The grass and asphalt were blue, and blue reflections moved on the hides of the three great Wilberforces gathered on the crater rim. Clumsily they began to slide down. Theo crawled forward and watched them. They moved like wool bales on a chute, in a lifeless way – yet Theo was not convinced. There was a pulsing in Lenart's light that had not been in Johan's. And he had not liked the way the stone had hovered as though uncertain of exactly where to drop. Johan had drawn a perfect arc.

The stone settled in the centre of the crater and a moment later the Wilberforces came to rest about it. They were still as three blocks of granite.

From the crater of Rangitoto a thin red beam of light climbed steadily into the sky. It bent towards Mount Eden, approached over the harbour, reached half way, and stopped: a red bow, bathing the sea and city in light. And slowly from the stone in Mount Eden's crater its companion began to grow. But it grew with such pain, such reluctance. It made ten metres, and fell back ten. It climbed again and fell. Watching, Theo knew that this was the damage he had done by putting Lenart down. The fault was his. If the blue arc of light failed to reach the red the world would die. He saw Auckland, a mass of lights, saw the buildings, the houses. The people would die, he would die, smothered in mud. The stars would go out.

The beam climbed again, fell back – not all the way. It stood like a blue spear fixed in the ground. Two more Wilberforces went by and slid down to join the others. The light climbed, with more ease Theo thought. It was taller than the crater rim and fell back only a third of its length.

The baby Wilberforces slid across the parking lot. They stopped beside Theo a moment almost as if to keep him company. Then they went down. The seven were there, about the stone, with blue light gleaming on their backs.

'Theo,' Rachel's voice said.

'Over here.'

She helped Mr Jones across the asphalt. The old man's face was grey. He sank to his knees beside Theo. The blue light shone in his eyes but he had no strength to speak.

The beam was climbing easily now. It began to curve towards Rangitoto. Although it stopped from time to time it did not lose any ground. And finally it was speeding like an arrow.

In the instant before it touched the red the Wilberforces gave a haunting cry like the distant fading call of trumpets. They turned away from the stone and gathered a little way off in a circle.

The beams met, ran along each other, the blue twining down into Rangitoto, the red to Mount Eden. And from their meeting place five woven threads ran out, to North Head, Mount Victoria, Lake Pupuke, to One Tree Hill and Mount Wellington. They touched — soil or stone or water. It was done.

At once the Wilberforces were gone. A fierce wet detonation sounded in the crater. And the mountain lurched. It seemed to heave itself into the air. A rumble sounded deep inside it. Half the southern rim of its crater slipped into the bowl with a shingly roaring sound, like a great spill of concrete. For a moment a huge force pressed from below and the asphalt round the place where the twins had fallen cracked like ice on a pond. The mountain trembled, trembled. It gave a groaning sigh. Then everything was still.

Slowly Rachel and Theo climbed to their feet. They looked about them. The lights of the city had gone out. Under the moon, the streets were ghostly, deserted. Only here and there the head-lights of a car sent out pale un-certain rays.

On the mountain the slip covered the place where the Wilberforces had exploded. The beams from the stones had vanished. In the air was a leaden hush, the stillness before some dreadful event. The twins felt their skin prickle.

Rachel gave a moan. 'Oh, no.' Theo covered his face. Then it came. The sky was filled with concussions, with cracking, with the scream of air torn apart. The sea buckled like tin. Over Rangitoto, over the lake, towers of fire and ash reared up like monsters in a dream. The sky turned to blood.

The twins held on to each other. A gale began to blow about their faces.

'What's happening?' Rachel wept.

It was a long time before Theo could answer. At last he said, 'The worms – they exploded. Because I couldn't hold Lenart.'

'But Rangitoto – the lake . . .?'

'It set them off again. The water got down to the lava.'

Rangitoto was not important, he knew. It would lay a foot of ash over the city. But the lake – the lake . . . All those houses, the hospital, the people . . . He hid his eyes and lay down on the ground.

'Theo,' whispered a voice.

He shook his head. 'Go away.'

'Your world is safe, Theo.'

He shook his head.

Rachel lay down beside him and put her arm over his back.

'My children, it is safe,' whispered Mr Jones. 'But you do right to grieve. That was the way it happened.'

His voice passed quietly through their minds. It died. They raised their heads and saw a pale flame floating over the crater. It turned into a mist. The wind broke it and flung it away.

In a little while they stood up. Under the fierce red sky they climbed down from the mountain and walked hand in hand through the streets. They found a knot of people and asked for shelter from the wind and ash.